"Joyeux Noël"

For Connie

You nurtured the first
seed of The Hideout!
Merci Mille fois!

Micheline DeCarrÉ

THE HIDEOUT

MICHELINE A. DeCAIRE

EDITED BY ALICJA POWER & JOCELYN TREPTE

authorHOUSE®

AuthorHouse™
1663 Liberty Drive
Bloomington, IN 47403
www.authorhouse.com
Phone: 1-800-839-8640

First published by AuthorHouse 11/2/2009

ISBN: 978-1-4490-1410-0 (e)
ISBN: 978-1-4490-1408-7 (sc)
ISBN: 978-1-4490-1409-4 (hc)

Library of Congress Control Number: 2009909947

Printed in the United States of America
Bloomington, Indiana

This book is printed on acid-free paper.

To Michael

CHAPTER ONE

The Planning

March, 1952.

A small boy stood silently at the grave, waiting for the people to leave to deposit his simple bouquet of wild spring flowers. He had gathered them in the field behind *La Madrague,* his family home, that morning.

He wiped his eyes on the frayed sleeve of his coat before kneeling down on the freshly dug earth. In the family plot, his grandmother, Anna, whom he never knew was buried. Close to her were his mother, Maria and his father, Nicolas.

Sophie gently squeezed his hand to pull him away.

"Come, Bambino, let's go back home," she said choking with sorrow.

"I want to talk to grandfather, *Fifi,*" he answered, calling her by the nickname he used for her since he was born.

"I'll wait for you over there," she said, motioning to the entrance.

Walking down the cemetery path, she mulled over the situation at hand. What now? What would become of that boy with Marius gone? Deep down, she new the answer. Marius had no other kinfolk.

The boy's undersized frame shook with grief, touching the earth.

"I miss you, *Oppa*. Why did you leave me here, all alone?" he said, sobbing.

Through a veil of tears, he noticed the little grave covered with tiny white roses on the other side of his grandfather. A marble angel with the open wings stood above the name engraved on the alabaster stone.

"Anne-Marie. Three years old. Sleeping with the angels in heaven," it said.

It was good that that little girl was buried close to his grandfather. It made him feel better. The angel would watch over his grandfather too.

The guttural cries of gulls whirling above broke the silence in the quiet cemetery on the hill above the sea.

On the way home, he thought of his grandfather dancing the Farandole at the Festival last summer, playing the usual game of *Petanque* with his friends and arguing about the score afterward.

Their argument always ended at the Plaza's café, and with sharing a glass of *Vin du Pays,* the special Rose wine of Provence.

The memory of his grandfather cut deep in the boy's tender heart.

Marius Santini had raised Niko since the day his only son, Nicolas Santini, along with his wife, Maria, failed to return from a secret mission for the Allies. This was to be their last dangerous mission for the Resistance movement during the war.

Long before the invasion of Normandy, June 6, 1945, thousands of French of all ages: men, women and children, joined the Resistance to fight for the freedom of their country.

Nicolas and Maria, were both embedded with a group of Partisans undercover helping the Allies to succeed in the "D Day" operation. On the eve of the liberation of Marseille, August 28, 1945, they were killed during a bloody battle in an ambush with the Nazis.

Their little boy was barely three years old.

Seven years later, when the fatal heart attack struck his grandfather, Marius, ten year old *Niko Santini* became an orphan overnight.

Sophie, known to Niko as "Fifi," a long time friend of the family, was Marius's housekeeper. She was now in her late eighties and in poor health. After the funeral, the good hearted woman cared for the boy until a further decision could be made.

Niko was born at *La Madrague,* his grandfather's estate which had belonged to the Santinis, who had been cultivating olive groves for generations.

The cottage in which Niko had lived with his grandfather was built on the foothills of the Mediterranean coastline in the outskirts of Marseille. Marius's woodworking shop, where he spent most of his days, was in the back.

It was there that he carved his *Santons,* colorful little wooden figurines so very popular in Provence.

People knew the quality of his work, and the fact that Marius put all his heart in his creation.

Early in his childhood, the boy became attracted to colors. He watched his grandfather brush paint on wood, wanting to learn more. At four, he knew most of all the colors by name.

"You see, Niko," Marius would tell the boy," this butcher must wear a white apron so he will look as if real in his shop.

"Why d' you paint the woman's dress in indigo, Oppa?" the intrigued child would ask him.

"Because color reflects the soul, the spirit, and the mind of a person, my boy," was his answer. "Without the right color, she would be incomplete, lacking perfection."

Marius taught the small boy to draw when he realized that he had a gift for it. He spent a lot of time, patiently describing art to his little grandson, who soaked up every word like a sponge.

Marius cultivated a small herb garden for medicinal purpose and for the making of his goat cheese. He had raised *Mimic,* his goat, since she was a kid, a companion at first, then, for Niko who had been raised on goat's milk.

The goat pen was next to the garden. It was quite a temptation for the stubborn goat who sneaked there every chance she could get. In no time, she would chew the tender greens to the roots.

Marius used some of his herbs, such as thyme or rosemary, to blend with the little, round goat cheeses that he sold at the market every week.

Three days after the funeral, when Niko was laying on his bed in the dark after dinner, he heard a loud knock at the front door. He didn't recognize the woman's voice talking with Fifi. Their voices were muted.

When his name was mentioned, his ears perked up at once. He quietly tiptoed to the ajar door of his bedroom to listen to their conversation.

"The boy must be ready early Sunday morning. The bus in Marseille will leave at 10:00 sharp for the orphanage," the woman told Fifi.

"I'll have him ready in time for you," was Fifi's curt answer.

Both women talked more but Niko wasn't listening anymore. His blood had turned to ice with what he had just heard. *Orphanage.* He knew about the orphanage. Children ended up there when they had no parents. They were going to send him there.

Panic overtook him but he started thinking of what to do next. He knew that he must get away from here before Sunday. For heaven's sake! He had to escape before they put him on that bus in two days. No way he was going to the orphanage!

After the woman left, Fifi went outside to milk and feed Mimic for the night. With a heavy heart, holding back his tears, he got his backpack from the closet. He had to get ready. Now.

He used to pack his bag when he and his grandfather, a naturalist at heart, took him on camping trips. Only this time, Oppa wasn't going with him, he would be on his own. Pushing back his tears once more, he went through his camping gear.

In the silence he heard the grandfather clock from the Grande Salle strike nine. How many times had he seen Oppa rewind it before retiring for bed?

The tears were almost there ready to spill. He pushed them back again, thinking of his next move. Maybe, what he should do, is to pack only what he need, and leave the rest for his suitcase.

Too much in his backpack would be too obvious. The first step was to decide where he would go without being caught.

He was still debating what to do when Fifi came back. Immediately, he jumped into his bed pretending to be asleep when she opened the door.

"Goodnight my Bambino, sleep tight," she whispered softly before closing the door.

All through the night, Niko contemplated the details of his plan, changing them often.

"I've got to go where nobody would look for me," he mumbled to himself.

"Like in the deep hills, ya, in the Calanques. There are hundreds of places to hide in the heavy bushes. Nobody would ever look for me there, they'd think I was still in the big city of Marseille," he thought.

"Marseille, the second largest city in France, is huge. It would take forever to find a kid in there," he thought. "I'll have to escape from the bus station, though."

In his mind, he tried to picture how it would happen at the bus station, weighing details back and forth.

"No matter what, I can't board that bus for the orphanage. Up in the deep hills is my best way, that's what I'll do," he thought.

Niko had camped many times in the Calanques with his grandfather. They used to take the popular trail from Marseille. Thinking about it, the boy thought that maybe it would be safer to take the trail from the other side of Marseille. From the east side, he'd climb the high hills.

Niko was sure that this would be the best way to go. He had made up his mind.

Then all at once, he deflated like a balloon when he realized that there was a big crack in his plan.

To reach the east side, he'd have to take a train from Marseille going east. The boy had never been on a train before.

"Where is the train station located?" he asked himself.

Once on the train, there would be no turning back. He'd have to find his way quickly before they discovered him and put him in the orphanage. His mind was going round and round. So many things could go wrong.

Could he do this without being caught?

CHAPTER TWO

The Escape

March 29,1952.

The Marseille bus station was noisy, crowded with people coming and going. The buses were leaving in every direction. Niko's chocolate brown, wide open eyes searched for the best way to escape before boarding his bus, due at any moment.

Impatiently, he brushed the lock of his raven black hair which had fallen over his eyes from under his crumpled blue cap. He stood next to the woman from the Children's Shelter.

She had barely talked to him since they left La Madrague. Niko thought that she looked weird, all dressed in black like a witch, even her black hat looked scary. Just as he had rehearsed it the night before, he kept his pack firmly on his shoulders.

He forced himself to look calm, act normal, desperate to run, he felt like jumping out of his skin.

Against a wall on his left, he saw a sign with an arrow pointing out the direction to the train station. Hey! What a brake! This was his chance.

"Just what I'm looking for, I've got to get there," he thought. Then, facing the woman reading her newspaper he asked her.

"I've got to use the bathroom before we get on the bus, M' am, I'll be right back, can you watch my suitcase?"

"OK, but hurry up, boy, the bus for Avignon will be here any minute," she answered before getting back to her reading.

Avignon! So that is where they were taking him to the orphanage. Fifi, wouldn't tell him when he asked her.

He left his suitcase purposely behind, then eagerly, ran in the direction of the train station. He knew she couldn't see him from where she was. He had to scram in a hurry.

Once he was outside, he saw the train station across the street. The depot was further down. He ran with all his might toward the depot, searching for a train going east. When a man at the gate looked right in his direction, his heart sank. He didn't have any ticket.

Someone from the crew called the man to discuss something, giving the boy the chance to slip across the track. Several boxcars, hooked to the locomotives were lined up to be loaded on the docking platforms.

One of the trains left the platform, showing the next boxcar would be ready to leave soon.

When another train left, Niko, by pure chance saw big letters written in chalk on the side of the next train. It made his heart flip: *Cassis.*

"Cassis! The Calanques, the wilderness, his way out," he thought.

A red signal flashed off and on at the end of the track where men loaded crates. The air smelled of carbon from the engines, huffing, puffing gray smoke, like colts ready to leave the barn.

He glanced both ways, being careful not to be seen by the crew ahead. He hid on the side of the track. Fortunately, they were too busy to see him. He counted fifteen boxcars.

The door of the last caboose was ajar.

His throat tightened. It was hard to breathe. When he hopped inside, he scratched his knees. Inside, wooden crates were piled on the top of each other. He crawled on his stomach underneath one of them in the far corner, waiting, hoping for the whistle.

Suddenly, he heard the crunch of some feet on the gravel close to the caboose.

"Gosh! Maybe they were going to load more crates in here," he thought.

His heart pounded so hard that he thought for sure they could here it from outside. He held his breath the best he could until someone slid his door shut.

Whoever was close by walked away. He heard faint voices, discussing load to go, and diminishing in the distance. He brushed his clammy hands on his pant leg. It seemed like hours to him, trembling, and being afraid people were already on his track.

Anticipating danger closing on him, he hoped with all his might that the train would leave soon.

When the whistle finally gave its blast, only then, the boy let a long breath out.

The engine snorted, jerked as the train started to move. The whistle gave a final signal. Then, second later the train was on the way. The boxcars shifted noisily, creaking on the rail.

It was dark inside with just a crack of light filtering through the door, it smelled like old dusty rags. The boy felt the caboose rolling under him with a grinding noise until the train picked up speed to an even tempo.

He slid his backpack down, trying to stretch his legs the best he could to ease his tensed muscles. The regular humming of the train soon made him sleepy. He hadn't slept much the night before while plotting his escape. Fatigue was catching up with him.

He remembered how Fifi had tried to explain to him why he had to leave, and sobbing while preparing his bags.

"Let's pack your clothes for your new home, Bambino," she told him.

You'll be OK, my Bambino. The orphanage will be a new start for you. It will be a new chance to meet children of your own age," she told the boy who was half listening.

Then, after blowing her nose a few more times, she added, "I wish I could keep you myself but I'm getting too old now. They wouldn't let me do that."

Niko thought she'll probably stay at La Madrague to look after the cottage and keep Mimic, too. He had no idea what would become of his grandfather's estate.

Early that morning, before leaving, it had been difficult for him to say goodbye to Fifi. She had been in his life since the day he was born.

She hugged him hard before putting a silver chain holding a medallion of the Virgin Mary, around his neck. Fifi knew how strong the boy was in his belief in the Blessed Virgin Mother. His grandfather had always taken the boy to church on Sunday.

"To keep you safe my Bambino," she said. You'll write to Fifi, you hear?" she insisted as tears rolled down her cheeks.

He had walked through the cottage before leaving, then went to hug Mimic outside. Before the woman had put him in the car, he looked back once more at La Madrague, his home, holding his tears as best as he could.

A loud whistle woke him up. He had dozed up. At first, he didn't know where he was and his mouth was as dry as cardboard. After a few seconds, he remembered everything. He crawled quickly from under the crates to slide the caboose's door open to take a look outside.

The *Calanques* stood right there in front of him like mighty cliffs, giants impressive fjords overlooking the blue Mediterranean. They were much more impressive than the cliffs he knew near Marseille.

"I've got to jump, right now, before they stop in Cassis," he told himself.

The train was still a way from the station, sending the final whistle before the stop. He set his backpack firmly on his shoulder to prepare himself.

When the train began to slow down, he took a long breath, leapt down, rolling on his side and landed hard on the ground. He looked both ways to make sure that there wasn't anyone around.

Cassis was about 30 kilometers east of Marseille. The cliffs were much higher on the east side, more prominent like big swords.

Good thing he wore his tennis shoes for the climb looked steep and rugged. The sun was already hot. He was sweating. He had piled on several T-shirts on top of each other to gain room in his pack.

He removed his sweatshirt to tie it around his waist. The young boy, confused and lost at first, searched for a path to climb through the wild area he had never been before. A bit further, he found a narrow path through the Allepo pines.

The further he climbed, the hotter he got, wanting to stop but not daring to do so, yet. He had to get higher, to feel safe before taking a break. Going through the rocky terrain became difficult and exhausting, but he kept going, looking around as he went, to the beautiful landscape.

Around him were all types of trees: Eucalyptus, silver-leaved olive trees, and dense maquis shrubs, some of them very aromatic. Among them were pretty white Cistus flowers. He smelled the myrtle shrubs. The sea lavender was just coming out.

He thought about his grandfather saying that Provence was indeed the land of the sun. Wild thyme grew in the rocky land, and the maritime pines looked like giant umbrellas with blue-tinged green needles that smelled wonderful.

Further up the hills, thirst got the best of him. Tired, he decided to stop to drink from the thermos Fifi had stuffed in his backpack that morning. He didn't know what she had packed in the brown sack that she handed to him before leaving.

"For the trip," she had told him, still sniffling into her handkerchief.

She used to do this kind of packing when he and Oppa went camping, filling their bags with all sorts of goodies. It was always a surprise for them, when they found everything later.

Checking inside the bag, he found chocolate bars, cookies, fruits, nuts and two cheese sandwiches. Niko sat in the pine shade to eat one sandwich and an apple, washed down with lemonade from the thermos.

From where he sat, he guessed that he had climbed quite a way from the train, maybe a couple of kilometers, maybe more.

He couldn't see the village yet, only part of the turquoise sea in the distance, beating against the reefs. Little fishing boats bobbed on the water. Down the hills, fragrant mimosa trees were in bloom, looking like a golden carpet. He wished he could just stay put because his legs felt tired.

He had camped enough with his grandfather to know that once the sun went down, it would be too late to find a place for the night. Oppa had made sure that he understood that after sundown, temperature dropped fast up in the hills.

He continued to climb the narrow path before coming to a fork, dividing two narrow paths, one going northeast, and the other northwest. Retrieving his compass from his back pocket, he decided to follow east, for any trail east from Marseille was much safer for him.

Revived by the food and the lemonade, he started to enjoy the climb. The birds chirped in the trees, happy about spring. Nature smelled freshly wonderful with the wild flowers covering the hills.

Further up, he had to slow his pace for the path became very dense with wild shrubs, almost impassable.

He thought he heard a noise, but the birds were making so much racket above his head, that he didn't pay attention to it. A little further, he heard it again and listened carefully. This time he was sure. It sounded like a muted dog's yap.

"What would a dog be doing here?" he questioned himself. Then, he became very still as it occurred to him: "Was the dog with someone?"

Instantly he was on his guard, afraid to be discovered, crawling under the bushes for cover. After a while, he couldn't see anyone around.

He was sure that he had heard yapping again. It was coming from the right side of him. Curious, he made his way toward the noise. A small mutt was digging frantically in the bushes, trying to get to something, probably a rabbit.

"What's he doing here in the middle of nowhere?" Niko thought.

When he whistled, the dog stopped to look at him, gave a little whine, then dug some more. As he approached the little creature with caution, the dog stopped, looked at him then went back to his digging.

He didn't wear a collar and other than looking very undernourished, he didn't seemed to be hurt in any way. Niko let him smell his hand to let him know he meant no harm. By then, he was pretty sure that the dog was alone.

"Did you follow me from down the track? What are you after in these bushes?" he asked the pooch. It was clear to him that the dog wanted to attract his attention. He was a cute little fellow.

Niko couldn't see anything at all at first, then, leaning closer, he saw what the little pooch was after. It looked like a hole entirely covered by dense, wild shrub brush, well hidden, almost impossible to see.

"What did you find in there?" he asked the pooch.

The dog wagged his tail, looking at him with his shiny eyes.

It took a while for Niko to clear the thick brush with his knife. This was much deeper than a rabbit hole. With the flashlight from his backpack, the boy tried to push his head through, slowly, in case there were any animals living in there.

The opening was lots deeper than he thought, almost like a cave. After clearing most of the brush, covering the entrance, Niko proceed to crawl inside cautiously.

Bears were well known to use caves as their lairs. Then, thinking about it, he realized that this hole covered with rocks and bushes was way too small for a bear.

"Stay right here," he said to the pooch, motioning it to stay in front. Like a little soldier, the dog sat right there guarding the entrance to the cave. Niko was amazed. Thanks to the stubborn yapping of this little mutt, he had found a cave carved in the stony cliff!

He looked around with his flashlight. All sorts of creatures big and small could be in here, but the boy couldn't see anything but rocky walls. A few minutes later, he called the dog to come inside.

"You've found us a real cave, pooch," he told the dog who was wagging his tail, looking at him with his brilliant brown eyes, proud as he could be.

"Nobody would ever find us here," he said, patting the dog's head.

"This is cool, the perfect hideout."

CHAPTER THREE

The Mysterious Cave

Niko checked around the cave carefully.

"What a stroke of luck! A cave! A real hideout in the wilderness for us," he exclaimed.

It was cooler in there and not as dark, once he made the entrance a little bigger to crawl inside. A thin sunray filtered through it, reflecting light on the limestone wall.

The Calanques, chiseled in solid limestone, were dazzling in their whiteness. Niko had read about grottos in the deep hills but had never seen one while camping with his grandfather. The boy thrilled with this discovery, made a quick inventory of his surroundings.

The pooch with is nose sniffed the ground, scratching the dirt here and there.

A strong smell of mildew impregnated the soil and the air. Other than that, the cave was tall enough to stand up in it.

Something got Niko's attention as he went around touching the walls. He felt a prickle at the back of his neck. In one corner against the wall, a moldy blanket was crumpled on the floor.

Why was that blanket there? "Was someone else in here?" His instincts went instantly into the state of alert, raising his hair. After a few seconds he realized that unless there was another entrance to the cave, nobody could be living in here with such a small hole to get in.

"I had to dug my way in, for heaven' sake!"

To reassure himself, he went back outside to look around this cave completely covered by rocks and bushed. He listened for sounds but couldn't hear anything but birds and cicadas.

"Perhaps an animal had dragged the old ragged blanket in there?", he pondered. Besides, he was sure that the dog would alert him if someone was next to the cave.

The sun was descending on the hills bringing the temperature down and the clouds looked like it could rain. The waif felt dead tired after this long and challenging day.

He took the blanket outside to shake it, beating it on the trees, and to make a bedroll for him and the pooch.

Sitting down, he opened his backpack to get the other cheese sandwich and some cookies to share with his new friend. In one of its back pockets, he found more chocolate bars, nuts and candies.

"Come sit here by Niko and let's eat something," he told the dog, tapping on the blanket, for the dog to sit.

"I've got to give you a name since you want to stick with me," he said petting him.

The mutt had an intelligent look about him. He put his front paw on Niko's leg. Probably this was his way to connect. It was clear to see that the little dog had already adopted Niko as his friend.

His coat was shiny black with tawny patches here and there, his four socks were white, as well as his underbelly and the tip of his tail.

His had a curious face, well marked, with a white strip between his sparkly brown eyes coming to the top of his head, as if someone had painted it on. The tip of his nose was black. Both eyes were lined in black, almost like a mask which gave him an inquisitive look.

Niko checked him all over again but couldn't see any cuts or sore spots. He thanked his Virgin Mother for sending the little dog to him. He would be a great friend and Niko sure needed one now!

"I know! Since you sniff, peck and scratch the ground as you do, I'll call you *Peco*! How do you like your name?" Niko asked. The pooch, wagged his tail, and came to lick the boy's hand in response. He seemed to understand every command the boy gave him.

After they finished eating, he went to sleep at the boy's feet.

Niko's eyes became heavy, gritty with fatigue, his entire body hurt, completely exhausted by the difficult climb, plus, the emotions of his escape. The apprehension of being caught had taking its toll. The loss of his grandfather came crashing on him all at once. He didn't know what would happen to him.

Surely by now, they had discovered his escape, and probably gone back to Fifi, searching, tracking for him, thinking he went back to La Madrague, his family home.

How was he to survive all alone? He didn't have much money with him. Only what was in his piggy bank. He felt a clutch somewhere in his chest thinking about his Oppa.

It had seemed so natural before to be together all the time. How was he going to get along without him? He never had the time to say good by to him. When Fifi came to get him at school that day, he had already passed away.

His Oppa was gone forever. He would never see him again.

The tears came down slowly at first, then steadily, spilling over the boy's cheeks, letting the grief out, cleansing his overflowing heart. The lonely orphan sobbed, crying himself to sleep on his bedroll.

Thunder woke him up during the night. He felt Peco's little body curled up against him, shivering. The pooch was scared.

Minutes later, he heard the raindrops falling on the rocky top of the cave, and then, pouring down, slapping on the stone cliffs above him. Lightning flashed through the bush at the entrance of the cave, like electric wires against the walls.

When the thunder cracked louder, Niko became frightened in this alien place. He wished that Oppa were here. Peco, sensing his fright, whined softly, licking the boy's face. The noise became deafening, lasting a long time.

When it finally quieted down, soft raindrops fell on the bushes, with the passing storm. Both, Niko and Peco were cold, with not much cover over them. Niko wished he hadn't been so exhausted last night and lighted a fire in the cave.

It was too late now. The wood would be too wet anyway.

Instead, he turned on his bedding, with his backpack as a pillow, holding Peco against his chest before both went back to sleep.

He woke up late the next morning, having no idea of the time. He looked for Peco but the dog was nowhere in sight. When Niko went outside to go to the bathroom, the sun was already high, probably close to noon. He whistled to call Peco but the dog didn't come.

Thinking he was somewhere chasing bugs, Niko went to look for dry branches to start a fire. He always had matches when he camped. He was just about to light the fire when Peco came out of nowhere to his side, holding something in his jaws.

"Where have you been? I looked everywhere for you, Peco."

"What d' you have here? Where d' you get this, le' me see?"

It was an old piece of rag, discolored by the weather, but Niko could see it had been red before. Checking it out, he noticed it looked like an armband with a strange black cross on it, two horizontal bars over one lateral bar.

"Where does this come from, Peco?" he asked becoming very curious. "Where d' you find this, show me?"

First, the old blanket, now this strange armband. What was all this about? The boy was puzzled.

The little dog yapped, wagging his tail, all happy with himself.

"Goodie, goodie," he had found something good, his master liked it. He gave another yap. Niko turned the armband over but could see no writing on it. Just the cross.

He lighted the fire inside the cave, still careful about being discovered, and then shared some cookies with Peco, before he decided to go investigate around the cave.

Maybe someone did come into the cave before, but why was it all covered up? He had seen no other signs inside. Just in case, he took a tour around the cave with Peco at his heels, circling the perimeter.

Niko couldn't see any tracks around. Something was puzzling about the armband. Maybe, someone did live in the cave before, but why was it all covered in stones with overgrown bushes at the entrance. He mulled this over for a long time while taking a tour up the hill.

Oppa had taught him during their camping to survive in the wilderness. He knew animal tracks, and which plant to use for tea. How to find wild edible onions, turnips, wild carrots and fennel. Also which medicinal plant to use for bug or snake bites.

Niko was excited to find fennel bulbs and rosemary, not too far from the cave. All he needed now was water to make hot tea. Further up hill, he saw hazelnut and apple trees. Neither fruits were ripe yet, nor the wild berries.

He picked some wild onions, a few turnips and the fennel bulbs. He wanted to cook them under hot ashes the way his grandfather used to do. His sandwiches were gone. He and Peco would be hungry, soon.

He knew that he should go down to the village to get bread but thought he should wait another day in case someone was looking for him there. The raw feeling of being apprehended sent his hair standing.

Orphanage was not a good outcome.

On his way back to the cave, he saw a few rabbit tracks. So, they were around here after all. He knew how to make traps but this would be for later. First things first: Water and bread.

Sitting on a rock next to the cave, Niko knew that there were springs draining from Mt-Puget in the Calanques but where? Mt-Puget was 1850 feet up in the mountain at its highest peak, way too high to go for water. His thermos was empty.

Maybe if he looked and searched around higher up hills, he could find a small spring. He was debating this when he heard Peco's yapping. It sounded to come from inside the cave. What was he into now?

By then, Niko came to recognize the difference between Peco's "*happy*" yapping and the "*I've found something*" yapping. This was definitely one "I found something" yapping.

Niko looked for him inside but couldn't see the little dog anywhere. He had been there just a minute ago. The boy looked around the cave, whistled for him, but no dog. This was getting very strange.

Niko whistled once more and listened. Peco's yapping was coming from the far left corner of the cave, but he couldn't see the pooch. Putting his ear against the wall, Niko heard water dripping inside.

After fetching his flashlight, he checked the wall, then, noticed a long gap in the corner he hadn't seen before in the darkness. It was big enough for the little dog to pass through. This was probably where Peco was before when Niko couldn't find him.

After pushing on the stone, to the boy's surprise, the wall rotated like on a pivot. Sure enough, Peco came out immediately. More confused by the minute, Niko passed through the gap to look inside.

It seemed as if there was a second chamber carved in the cave. Checking further with his light, what he discovered was stunning.

The chamber was long and narrow, almost like a tunnel with a lower ceiling than the cave and no opening at all. Therefore, it was dark inside. When he touched the wall it was wet. Spring water trickled through the rocky stone.

Somehow, the little mongrel had found it. Niko was amazed.

Shinning his flashlight around him, he saw some rusty electrical wiring on the dirt floor, and tools in a wooden box. In one corner there was a stack of musty blankets, like the one he had found piled up against the wall. Big letters "US" were marked on them.

Some pots and pans and cardboard cases with the same "US" stamped on them were piled up. In the back of the chamber stood a large wooden opened wine barrel. It was full of cartridges like the ones the hunters used in the fall for hunting birds.

Niko remembered picking up the empty cartridges behind La Madrague. On the dirt floor in the center of the chamber was some residue of burned wood, as if someone had built a fire there. Two lamps with a five gallon of oil were close by.

Niko saw more armbands with the same cross. He was baffled. All this stuff was old, very old. The boy couldn't understand who had been in here long ago. Perplexed, he went to get his thermos to fill it with water.

The fine dripping was coming steady. At least they would have water. He could make tea with the rosemary he had gathered before. Niko took one of the dip pots and washed it under the spring.

Dragging one heavy cardboard case underneath the spring, he put the pot on it to collect water. He washed the vegetables before putting them to cook under the hot ashes. Afterward, more confused than ever by what he had found, he went back in the chamber to check what he could use among the pots and pans.

It was then that he noticed wrinkled newspapers in a corner on the dirt floor. He hadn't paid any attention to them before. Bringing his light closer, he saw that the newspapers were old, yellowed, and dirty. The text was in a language he couldn't read at all.

On one of the crumpled pages, was a picture of a tall man wearing a uniform with lots of medals on his chest. Niko realized the same cross on his lapel was similar to the cross on the armbands. Who was this man?

The boy became more curious by the minute, quickly looked through the pages trying to understand. Then suddenly his heart came to a standstill.

Looking closer with his light, he stared at another picture on another page. This wasn't possible. His heartbeat accelerated. His small hands started to shake as he read the writing once more, staring at the picture on the soiled newspaper.

He ran to his backpack to fetch something in one of the pockets. Something that followed him everywhere he went. The dog-eared picture of his parents, smiling. His beautiful mother wore a flowered dress, holding his father's arm.

Her black curly hair was a sign of her Spanish ancestry. Around her neck, she wore the same medallion that Fifi had given to him before he left.

In the photo, his father had Oppa's smile. He wore an open- collar shirt, and holding Maria, tenderly. Oppa had given that picture to the small boy a long time ago when he told him about his parents.

Niko cherished it with whole his heart.

The shaking boy looked intently at the picture on the newspaper once more to focus on the big letters underneath. *Nicolas Santinis.*

That was his father's name printed under the picture. Nicolas Santinis was his father.

What his papas picture was doing in here?

Had his father been in this cave?

Why? When? And what was his father doing here?

CHAPTER FOUR

A Friend

Niko heard the faint church bells in the distance the next morning when he was searching for wood. Their crystal clear sound reminded him of going to church with Oppa on Sunday. After church, they used to go to the market, where his grandfather sold his goat cheeses.

The young boy would go from stall to stall to check the juicy melons and delicious fruits. He never failed to stop at his favorite stand to watch an artist paint sceneries from Provence on his easel. He wished that he could do that.

While the boy was gathering the wood, a strange longing to visit his Blessed Mother filled his heart. Maybe he should descend below to the village to see the church. He also hungered for hot crusty bread. Wild edible onions were Ok, but he wanted fresh melon.

He had lost track of the days since his escape. If today was Sunday, the market would be opened on the plaza.

"Every village in Provence has a market, why not Cassis?" he thought.

Niko had never been to Cassis before. It was time to see it.

He felt safer in this part of the Calanques, hoping that by now the authorities would have given up looking for him. If they had not, they

23

would never think that he took a train out of Marseille. Of course, he must be careful before venturing into the crowd.

"The heck with it, we're going down to the village," he mumbled to himself. The money he had in his bag could buy food for a few days but it wouldn't last long. He should look for some small job.

"After all, I'm responsible for Peco now. He belongs to me."

In his loneliness, he was proud to have someone of his own to care for. the dog was part of his life now.

"We're going down to the village, Peco, he told the pooch who was always on his heels. You and I, have to find food."

The pooch shook his tail and gave a little yap to approve of the idea. It was fascinating to see how well they understood each other. Niko often wondered where this little dog came from and was thankful he came to him.

And so, on that bright afternoon, they started their descent to the village. Niko had to get himself oriented to be able to get back to the cave. Oppa taught him often to make landmarks when they were in the wilderness gathering herbs.

He selected several flat rocks and piled them on the top of each other, marking direction with branches.

Peco might be able to smell the cave, but he didn't want to take any chances.

The way down the hills seemed easier that when he came up from the train. From up high, in the distance, he could see the Mediterranean Sea to guide him.

"I can't get lost if I keep my eyes on the sea, right?" he told Peco, who was sniffing trees along the way.

During the hot summer months from May to September, the tourists trails in the Calanques are closed for fear of fire. But this was early spring, and he could meet someone on the way. The closer he got to the village the bigger was the panic that took hold of him.

He breathed deeply, inhaling the fresh air of spring, letting his mind wander. Thoughts of what he had found in the cave nagged at him.

"Why was papa's picture there?" It was troubling him a great deal. He didn't know how he was going to find the answer, although he wouldn't stop trying.

"When we are in the village I don't want you to wandered around, just stick with Niko," he told the mutt. "If I say, sit, you sit Peco, you don't move, you hear?"

Marking his directions with stones and logs along the way, they arrived at the cross-trail Niko had found the day he came from the train. He went west some distance, and soon could see a church's steeple above the pine trees. Further on he saw a marked trail going to Cassis.

He turned to look back up hill and estimated that it was about three kilometers to return to the cave. He did well to mark the way, since it would be really easy to get lost in the dark climbing back after sundown.

"I'll have to make better markers later on," he decided.

The west trail ended at a slope going down behind a little church. It descended to the village, then about two blocks to the sea. The pretty little church was built in limestone with Roman architecture.

Niko wanted to see it, but before entering he turned to the dog.

"Wait for me right here, don't move Peco, you hear?" he told the dog, and removing his cap to put it in his pocket. The little pooch gave a whine and sat at the front of the church as he was told.

Above the wooden domed portal, there was a stone statue of a smiling angel unfurling its wings like if welcoming anyone entering the doors. At its feet was an inscription. *"Sainte Marie des Pêcheurs."* (Sainte Marie for the fishermen)

Niko crossed himself and moved to the front. It was cool inside and very quiet. A few women with heads covered in black lace were seated on the right praying the Rosary.

Coming from the bright sun, the boy waited a few seconds to adjust his eyes to the darkness inside. Looking around, he saw what he was looking for. The Virgin statue was in the left wing.

Her garment was painted in white and gold. She had a pale blue veil on her head while holding her child in her arm. Roses sprang up at her feet.

The orphan knelt in front of her, crossing himself a second time and kissing his medallion before asking her forgiveness for escaping and thanking her for Peco.

The sunray filtered though the stained glass window, bathing the church inside with a multitude of colors, dancing like jewels on the altar. The golden cross placed on it shone with the reflections.

Ever since he was a toddler, Niko always was fascinated with stained windows.

He was glad that he came, for he felt safe in front of his Blessed Mother. Bowing his head, he asked her to help him.

"Please, Blessed Mother, can you help Niko? I'm afraid without my Oppa," he prayed.

He watched the candles flickering on each side of her when a sound behind him made him turn his head.

"It's always nice to see children praying," said a gentle voice. "I'm Father O'Mally, welcome my son, what should I call you?"

"I'm Niko, Father."

"I don't remember seeing you in school, Niko, are you from Cassis?" asked the young priest, sitting next to him.

Taking by surprise, Niko became mute at first, then recovered seeing the smiling face.

"I'm not from here Father, I never been to this school. Niko comes from far away," he answered feeling sure of himself now.

"Are your parents visiting our little village?"

"No! My parents are dead, I live with my grandfather. Today I came here alone," he replied while his heart beat accelerated, waiting for the next question.

"Perhaps I will meet him." Father O'Mally said with a smile, watching the boy.

Something in the quick answers told him to stop prying. This little boy's furtive look made him curious.

"Why don't you come have a bit to eat with me, Niko,?

I've got some nice Pistou soup on the stove, you can keep me company if you've got the time"?

Soupe au Pistou, the magic words. How good it would be to eat this after what he and Peco have been eating for several days.

"Sure, Father, I'll like to come but I have my dog waiting outside."

"Bring him along, what's his name?" asked the priest.

"I call him Peco because he always pick the ground like a chicken," Niko answered.

Father O'Mally could sense that something was different with this boy. The dirty, crumpled, clothes told him that Niko wasn't wealthy. His deep chocolate eyes and raven black hair told him that he came from Spanish ancestry.

"Come on, Niko, follow me," he said after closing the church door, while the small pooch approached to sniff his cassock.

"Well, you must be Peco, welcome!" he said patting the dog's ears.

Niko smelled the soup aroma the second he entered the kitchen, which made his mouth water and his stomach growl.

"Grandfather used to make that soup," he said, not realizing that his tongue had slipped into the past tense. "I love it!"

Father O'Mally had caught the slip but remained quiet. He wanted the boy to feel at ease with him. He had worked with vagrants before.

"The good Sister made it for me, I didn't. I'm not a very good cook. Sit down my boy and let's say prayer."

With the first mouthful, Niko thought that he was in heaven. He dipped the crusty bread in the soup that was offered. The Father gave a dish to Peco on the porch.

The youngster ate ravenously, taken a second helping without hesitation. He didn't know how hungry he was until he tasted the first mouthful.

"Tell me Niko, where is your grandfather now, and what is he doing?" the young priest asked tentatively after the boy had filled his stomach.

Niko thought a few seconds before answering. He didn't want to tell a lie to Father. At the same time, he had to be careful.

"He used to be a woodcarver, making Santons of Provence. He was the best Santons maker in Marseille. Now he sleeps all the time," said Niko, catching himself, not daring to look at the priest.

"I knew a great woodcarver once who made Provencal Santon in Marseille. His name was Marius," Father O'Mally said looking in his brown eyes. He caught the frightening look in the waif's eyes just in time. It was the look of a frighten prey before its predator.

"The boy was in trouble all right, but what for?" he thought, hesitant to ask further questions. Then Niko stood up.

"I must go now, Father. Thank you for the great dinner. Peco and I must go to the market get some fruits."

"You must come see me again, Niko, soon. I love to get to know you better. Perhaps you and I can talk some more the next time."

"Sure, Father, I'll come back to see you. Bye Father."

"I hold you to that. Bye Niko, take care, and you too Peco." He waved as they were leaving. The boy is definitely holding something back," Father O'Mally thought, closing the door.

Niko likes that young priest with the smiling face and wished he could stay longer, but first he and Peco must hurry to the market before climbing back to the Hideout.

The boy thought for a minute about the Father's questions before turning toward Peco.

"Can we trust him, Peco or is he going to give me away?" he asked his friend.

CHAPTER FIVE

Gus

Traipsing along the old port with Peco, Niko enjoyed his freedom. Bare feet in the water, he watched colorful little fishing boats bobbing on the turquoise sea. Some of the boats were blue, other green, yellow, or red, which made them part of the Mediterranean scenery.

The fishermen were busy mending their nets on the pier, talking with each other about their catches. He thought again about Father O'Mally, who new his grandfather. Niko was afraid. He must be careful of what he said to him. Yesterday after leaving the priest, Niko had gone to the market to look for half-priced melons. It would be cheaper so late in the day.

The Fish Market was located Place des Pêcheurs by the port. It reminded him of the noisy atmosphere in Marseille.

The familiar *criée* from the fishmongers resounded throughout the market.

"Come see my belle sardines, Madame," yelled one woman.

"Over here, fresh crab, the best catch of the day," yelled another.

Other than fish and seafood *"a Go-go,"* some stalls were filled with garlic, tomatoes, colorful peppers, beans, goat-cheese, vegetables, fruits, herbs of Provence, and buckets of olives of every category.

Niko could smell the succulent aroma of the melon in his backpack and the hot crusty bread he had bought at the *boulangerie.* He saw paper flowers hanged in the tiny shops all through the village.

Cassis was ready for the coming Saint Patrick Festival. A few men were preparing the music stand for the band. Niko wanted to see the folkloric dances on the plaza, for sure.

He had no problem finding his way back to the hideout with his markings.

"But there might be a shorter way to go to Cassis," he thought to himself.

Sitting by the sea, Niko mulled over what he had seen, when a man carrying a net on his shoulder approached him. He was unshaved, rough looking, with is belly spilling over his belt, didn't seemed to be starving.

"Hey kid! Doing nothing? You want make a few buck? I need help to clean fish and wash the deck," he said in a loud voice.

Cool! Just what Niko was looking for. Perhaps not this soon, but he needed a job. Clean fish, wash the deck? No big deal! This was a brake.

"Sure! I can do that, I want to earn money for the festival, Sir"

"Call me Gus. Get your butt on the boat. See that bucket of fish? Grab the scaler next to it and start cleaning!" he told the boy roughly, dumping the net on the boat before he disappeared below.

Niko wasn't sure about the man but he did need a job.

"Peco, you stay where you are. Don't wander around like you always do. You wait for Niko, right here where I can see you, you hear?" he told the dog before stepping on the fishing boat.

It was far from new. Of medium size with the green paint mostly gone.

The boy worked the whole afternoon. The sun was just melting into the sea when he finished hosing the deck.

With his fingers, Niko brushed the wild lock of dark hair falling in his eyes, before calling Gus down below.

"Gus, I'm done with my work now," he said wanting to get pay.

The man came up from below with a bottle in one hand, then handled Niko a handful of change with the other. It wasn't much, but enough to get bread and maybe a slice of cheese.

The orphan had missed Oppa's cheese since his escape. In fact, he had missed his cooking a lot. His grandfather was a great cook, especially his good *Bouillabaisse* or his famous ratatouille. They often had this with crusty bead for dipping on Sunday, after coming back from church.

When he came home from school, Oppa always had a snack of bread and cheese with a glass of milk waiting on the table.

"Eat Niko! It'll make you strong," was his often repeated saying.

"Gee! I sure miss that," he thought sadly to himself. Then, he remembered school. It seemed so far away. He used to love school until that terrible day. It was a day that changed his life, bringing his whole world crumbling down.

Oppa was gone forever. He was all alone now.

It was almost dark by the time they got back to the cave. After he built the fire and prepared something to eat, he was tired. He had worked hard. Although he was small and skinny, he was strong for his age.

He was sipping hot tea from the tin cup he had found in the cave when his eyes stopped on the limestone wall. The flames from the fire danced on it, swirling different shapes. Suddenly, Niko thought of something.

"Why didn't I see this before?" he said aloud standing up. Walking up to the wall, he grabbed a piece of charcoal from the ashes. His fingers stroked the white wall as if it was made of velvet.

Studying the dancing flames that reflect on the grooves more closely, he followed the undulating waves made with the charcoal carefully.

He stood back to look at it from a distance, then touched the wall again with his fingers. His lines formed waves on the ocean. He stroked the rugged wall to feel its relief texture similar to a three dimensional effect.

A new eagerness came over Niko as he reacquainted himself with his art. In his loneliness after his grandfather death, this was what he missed the most. Oh! How he missed this. His love for art was part of him, engraved in him, step by step, by his grandfather from an early age.

With the help of the lanterns found in the chamber, he worked on the wall a long time that evening. The limestone being porous made it possible, as he discovered, to erase his mistakes quickly with a damp rag.

Checking and rechecking his drawing, the small, grubby hands, worked swiftly. Niko followed patiently with each groove in the wall to create a scenery in his mind. Overwhelmed by what he did, he turned to Peco.

"What do you think of this, Peco my friend," he asked to the pooch, already snoring by the fire.

Still talking to the dog from time to time, he worked until his eyes became blurry. Then, he fell asleep flat on his bedroll.

Niko had always been an early riser. He woke up with the sunrise the next morning ready to go. Gus expected him to come early for the fishermen were coming back from the sea loaded with fish.

He wore the only dirty pants that he owned. He didn't have many T-shirts to spare either. His clothes were wrinkled from being in his backpack. He wore his tennis shoes without socks, working barefoot on the boat with the wet floor.

Cleaning fish was a tedious, dirty work. Washing the deck was much easier. After a few days he got the hang of it. Gus gave him his money after work each evening. It didn't take long for Niko to find out that Gus favored the bottle.

One evening at dusk, Niko stopped hosing the deck, bloodied from guts and fish's scales to watch a boat sailing into port. With her three sails flapping in the wind, she was a beauty. Gus, emerging from below with a bottle in one hand, came at him screaming, swearing in a slurred voice.

"You good for nothing, what's you looking at? What I'm paying you for? Get back to work before I belt you one," he exploded, making a gesture to remove his belt.

Niko got frightened. Oppa had never hurt him in any way. He got up on deck, trembling for the rest of that evening. He was glad to get back to the hideout and to relax by drawing.

The next day, Gus acted as if nothing had happened so Niko did his work quietly, but he made sure to avoid Gus when he was drank.

One morning following Peco who was chasing a rabbit, Niko found a short cut to the village. The best part about it was that it went straight to the slope from another angle. It was practically impossible to see the cave or his tracks through the dense brush.

"Cool! It occurred to him he could go unnoticed.

Every time he left the cave or when he came back at night, he always made sure to cover the cave's entrance with a large bush. With the tools found in the cave, he had made a door-like object which covered the hole completely. The hideout was his home now, his refuge.

Niko was almost sure that no one came near the cave, in case that someone might wander nearby, he still was careful. The popular trails and footpaths going through the Calanques were on the other side of the hill, away from him.

The mighty cliffs good for mountain climbers were located by the Cap Canaille, west of Cassis, with the highest point reaching1310 feet.

The Calanques Massif stretched for almost thirty miles between Marseille and Cassis. Several roads from Marseille led up to the great Mont Puget, about 1850 feet high at the peak.

Niko has seen these roads before when camping with his grandfather but had never been to the summit. From there, springs came down through the hills. Probably the one sipping in the cave's chamber was one of them.

Niko and Father O'Mally bumped into each other at the market one afternoon.

"Hi! there, Niko. Nice to see you, my boy. You too Peco," he said, petting the dog on the head. Peco recognized him by sniffing his cassock.

"Bonjour! Father. Can I help you to carry one of your baskets? Niko asked eager to help.

"You may. Actually I'm glad to see you, I was hoping to run into you, Niko. I like your help for the Festival Sunday afternoon. Can you do it?" "It would do me a great favor," he continued.

"Sure, Father, I don't work on Sunday. I'm planning to go to the festival too. What can I do?

"Come with me to the Presbytery and I'll tell you," he said while the boy took one basket full of vegetables from his left hand.

"Bless you, my boy, let's go. We can have supper together if you like. I think the sisters cooked a great *Bourride* today."

Father O'Mally knew that this waif didn't eat well, so the bait to bring him to the kitchen worked, and he could use him for the Festival.

"Working! where in the world is this small boy working?" he though as they reach the Presbytery.

"Why don't you wash your hands over there in the sink while I set the table, Niko," he told him.

Niko was ashamed to look so grubby at the Father's table. Although he washed his face in the morning at the spring, he did need a bath and some grooming. He had tried to wash some of his T-shirts, soiled by fish blood, but he didn't have any soap.

After the second helping of the thick Bourride made of fish soup, beans and vegetables, Niko, felt full. He sure liked to eat here.

"This is a real good soup, Father," he said, finishing his crusty piece of bread and giving a piece left over to Peco, who was sitting at his feet expectantly.

"I'm glad that you like it, Niko. Have an apple." The Father said.

"Now, Niko, this is what I would like you to do for me. Sainte Marie will have a booth for the Saint Patrick Festival Sunday. Sister Agnes will need help in the afternoon. Can you serve lemonade?"

"Ya! I can do that, I know how to pour lemonade, Father," the boy answered him, smiling and brushing his wild lock of hair off his eyes.

"Well! Then, that's settled. I'll be counting on you Sunday after church, Niko. You will have time to go see the Farandole dancers," the priest added.

"Sure thing! I bet it's cool to see them all dressed up in their costumes. Thanks for the soup," Father, I got to go now, "the boy said, getting up.

The young priest watched him leave with the same thought he had had the last time.

"Where does this kid spend the night? Perhaps in a few days I'll find out. Will I learn more about this mysterious boy?"

Chapter Six

The Festival

The minute Niko reach the church, he could feel the festival excitement in the streets. After attending mess, he met Father O'Mally as he had promised.

The night before, Sister Agnes and Father O'Mally had prepared several baskets for the Sainte Marie booth at the *Festival*. Niko helped them load everything on the cart. The Saint Patrick Festival was a grand event in Cassis every year. People of all ages looked forward to it.

Used to be ever alert since his escape, Niko instantly scrutinized the crowd.

"Would someone be here to recognize him?" he feared.

The festival was located at the Place des Pêcheurs where the market usually took place.

The joyous atmosphere filled every street. Colorful green paper banderoles hung in the windows or above the doors of houses, which gave the little village a festive look.

Sister Agnes gave Niko her instructions to serve the lemonade from a large basin covered with floating lemon slices on top. Paper cups were piled up next to it.

Father O'Mally was ready to leave for the *Blessing of the Sea* as Sister Agnes prepared several trays with little *Navette* pastries. Everyone loved the boats-like pastry, a Provence specialty. No Festival was complete without it. Other booths served *Fougasse,* an olives-flavored bread.

Next to their booth, a woman sold *Pan-bagnat,* bread rolls, filled with tuna, olives, and tomatoes, pressed down to blend the flavor. Others booth sold *Pissaladière* pizza. All profit from the festival was going to charity.

The famous *Calissons Bonbons* candies with almonds and sugar were sold almost everywhere. Coming from Marseille, Niko was quite familiar with everything he saw around him. His mouth watered at the thought of eating some of the treats. Everything smelled so good.

The Saint Patrick festival opening was led by Father O'Mally who performed the *Blessing of the Sea.* This was accomplished by people walking in the water with the Virgin Statue standing on a platform covered with flowers, supported by six men.

During the procession, the priest cassock got wet at the bottom. This religious ritual was performed every year to bless the water and to protect fishermen at sea should a storm put them in peril. It was also to ensure that they would come back with an abundance of fish.

After the blessing came the parade in the streets with the band, followed by all the dancers performing the *Farandole.*

Each of them was dressed in their traditional costumes of Provence.

As soon as the parade was over, people came rushing to the booths. Niko was busy serving his lemonade with Sister Agnes at his side. She took care of serving pastries and receiving the money.

Children ran from one booth to another, excited to be there and watching clowns doing all kinds of tricks for them.

The previous week the Sisters at the Presbytery had found clean clothes for Niko to attend church on Sunday. He felt great wearing his new clothes for the festival.

His eyes trained at evaluating colors, were always mystified by the characteristic Provencal patterns. The colorful motifs blended in the traditional costumes, the long striped skirts with deep purple aprons, and *Capelino* on the women's head interested him. The younger girls wore white laced coifs with long ties floating in the breeze.

The men's costume was less colorful.

Their white shirt knotted at the collar by black ribbon was covered by a dark-colored vest. They wore black trousers with wide belts and on their heads, black felt hats with wide brims. The watch chain hanging from their pockets grabbed everybody's attention.

At three o'clock, the crowd made their way toward the plaza to see the dance exhibition. The dancers aligned themselves two by two to prepare for the dance.

"Why don't you go watch the dancers, Niko. I'll watch the booth. Go ahead!" Sister Agnes told the boy, who was full of curiosity. Niko saw the *"Farandole"* a Mediterranean dance dating way back from the Middle Ages.

Young men and women held on to one another by the corner of one handkerchief and danced to a six-beat rhythm.

The *Tambourinaires* played a typical Provencal instrument called the *Galoubet,* a sort of flute which produced a piercing sound.

The other instrument they used was the *Tambourin,* a type of drum made from calf-skin. It seemed to Niko that the music made by the *Chanterelle,* another instrument equally popular, imitated the singing of the cicada so frequently heard in Provence.

While all this was going on, a little further on, some older men played their game of Pétanque. The game was fun for Niko to watch, especially when the players get very excited, shouting and gesturing about the ball landing too close or too far.

When his time to help was over, Niko walked through the festival grounds checking the booths, each serving different things. He had left Peco that morning in the Presbytery.

His mischievous pooch had the bad habit of wanting to sniff everything. It was better to leave him behind just in case. Who knows what he would get into?

He had very little money with him which he had saved from his wages. Sister Agnes had put some Navettes in his pocket, and later he bought some Pan-bagnat.

He liked the Fishing Pond the best. This was neat! People, mostly children, with a fishing pole tried to catch a prize floating on the water. It was fun to watch. He wished he hadn't spent all his money on food.

He sure would like to try for the marbles. The cobalt marbles hypnotized him, but he had just enough change left to buy some *Barbe a Papa,* (Cotton candy)

He liked the colorful pistachio.

While eating his treat, he sat on the sidewalk in front of the Wine Tasting tent. He watched couples wearing the traditional costume of Provence dance to the music.

Niko enjoyed them for a while longer before making his way back to the booth. Father was back helping Sister Agnes to pack up. He looked at the boy, grinning at the sight of the cotton-candy stick in his hand.

"Stay longer if you want, Niko, enjoy the Festival. Make sure to come back before sundown," he added, hoping that he could keep this mysterious boy, safely overnight.

"Thanks, Father. I'd like to see everything. It's cool. I'd like to go back to the fish pond to watch people get prizes. I couldn't take part of the game for I didn't have any money left. I used it all on this," he said, motioning his treat.

"Here, Father O' Mally said searching in his cassock's pocket for some coins. This is for your help at the booth, Niko. Have fun. I'll watch Peco," he added.

Gee! Thanks, Father, I hope that I can catch those blue marbles. They're real net! See you later," he said already running toward the fish pond while Father O' Mally shook his head.

"Niko, Niko, what I'm I going to do with you?" he mumbled to himself.

Niko passed people watching a juggler throwing balls in the air and doing a pirouette before catching them again.

Another crowd were rooting strong men flexing their muscles power with a heavy hammer, boasting to could reach the highest marking.

The sun was going slowly down when the boy walked back to the presbytery. He was fingering the satin marbles in his pocket. He had missed the first time but by golly, he got his prize after the second try.

"Whoa!" he said, remembering the beauty of everything he had seen.

"If only I could draw those colors on the wall."

Father was disappointed when Niko refused to stay for the night.

"Me and Peco, we better get back before night," he said without telling Father why. He had never stayed out so late. He hoped that he could found his way back in the dark.

"By the way, how is your grandfather, Niko, when will I meet him?" the priest asked before the boy opened the door.

"He sleeps a lot, so Peco and I, let him rest," he answered, avoiding Father O' Mally's eyes.

He had the bluest eyes that Niko had ever seen. The boy was sure that they could penetrate through him and see the lie beneath.

"Isn't he well? Perhaps I could go visit him," Father O' Mally insisted tentatively.

"Grandfather is doing OK. It's better to leave him alone. Maybe someday you can come with me to visit him," answered Niko, stepping outside.

Father O' Mally didn't miss the boy's distant look or the tears in the corner of his eyes. They were there, almost ready to spill, but the waif, controlled himself at once.

"I've got to go now. I must be back before night. Bye, Father, and thanks for the coins. I had a really good time at the festival."

Father closed the door, thoughtfully.

"Where does this boy live, where does he sleep at night? Is he in bad trouble? I must find out. There must be a way to help Niko," he thought, knowing the boy wasn't going to school.

He had seen enough errant boys in his lifetime to know that something wasn't quite right with Niko. Although Father didn't want to admit this to himself, he had a soft spot for the urchin.

There was something about the boy that he wished to learn more about. He was suffering, this much was clear. The suffering was evident, but why?

Chapter Seven

Pierre

A crimson sunset descended over the Mediterranean just as Niko finished his work. Since the day Gus had showed his true temper, the boy carefully stayed out of his way when the man was drinking, which was often.

On his way back from the boulangerie, up ahead he saw an elderly woman dressed in black with a laced fichu on her head. She carried a basket that seemed quite heavy in her right hand. In her left hand, with difficulty she held her cane to balance herself.

She leaned down on it so much that Niko thought that she was going to fall on the ground.

"Here, let me help you, ma' m," he offered, taking her basket. "Where d' you leave? I can carry this for you?" he continued.

"Well! Thank you my lad, I sure could use yo' help. I leave right across from that restaurant, over yonder," she told him, motioning. Niko saw the sign immediately.

"What a nice thing to do for an ol' woman like me," she told Niko as they reached her house. She pushed a wooden gate to enter a small garden in front of the house.

"Come inside, lad, I'll fetch you something for yo' help," she continued while opening her door with a key.

"Oh! No, m' am. I don't need money. Thank you. I hope that I can help you again some day," he answered pushing the coins away. He watched her toothless, wrinkled face thinking of FiFi, which he had missed terribly since his escape.

"Ok! then, but take this," she insisted, handling him some cookies wrapped in paper.

"Thanks for the cookies, ma' m, I'll see you. Bye," Niko told her when leaving her house. He whistled for Peco as he closed the garden's gate.

"Hey kid! Come over here for a minute," said a man, sitting in the back of the restaurant, across the alley, smoking a cigarette.

He was of large stature, dressed in white with a long apron tied around his bulky waist. His reddish, chubby face smiled when the boy approached him. Peco, off course, went to sniff his apron.

"I watched you carrying *Annie*'s load a while ago. It's mighty decent, kid. Old Annie there, she shouldn't carry stuff like this. She's going to fold in half, one of this day." the man said.

"Ah! It's Ok. I like to help people," Niko answered him as the tall man was getting up from his chair.

"What's your name, kid? I never saw you around here before. Come inside have a glass of lemonade with me. I'm Pierre, the Chef of *"La Ratatouille,"* he said, pushing the boy inside with his large hands.

"I'm Niko. I never talk to a Chef before."

Then, looking around at all the pots and pans hanging from the ceiling, he continued,

"Gee! That's a big kitchen, you've got. It sure smell good in here."

This small kid with the strong Spanish look interested him. He seemed smart as a whip. "A stray kid for sure if I ever saw one," Pierre though to himself, watching the unruly black hair falling over the cap.

"God! This kid is skinny as a rail," he noticed.

"Why don't you sit down, Niko, let's know each other a bit while I'll pour you a cool drink?" he said, as Niko checked the place out.

La Ratatouille was a big restaurant. On the large terrace, facing the Mediterranean, tables were set with checkered blue and white tablecloths and vases of fragrant mimosa in the center.

Several cooks were busy preparing food on the stoves for the evening dinner. Niko didn't miss a thing while sipping his lemonade.

"I bet you cook some cool dishes. My grandfather was a great cook too," he said. "I miss his Bouillabaise a lot." The boy had a far away look in his eyes.

"Where is your grandfather now, Niko?" the Chef asked the boy in a soiled shirt.

"He is sleeping now".

"I work on a fishing boat on the old port for a man called Gus. You know him?" Niko said changing the subject quickly.

"You work for Gus? Gee! Niko, watch him my boy, he has a nasty temper when he drinks," the Chef told him.

Pierre had witnessed Gus violent temper once when he was drunk. He had punched a guy to a pulp in an alley behind the "Bar de la Marine". He was out of his mind and would probably have killed his victim if someone hadn't separated them.

"Yap! I already find that out a few days ago, but I'll be careful," Niko answered.

Then, standing up to go, pushing the chair back, Niko continued:

"What's you're cooking today, Chef Pierre, that smell so good?"

"Today, our special is *Moules Mariniere*," Pierre answered, scratching his head.

"Tell you what, you want to take some pizza home with you, Niko," he asked, thinking that this skinny kid needed food in his stomach. Good grief, he was bony.

"Sure! I'll like that, I never turned down pizza, Chef Pierre, me and Peco we love pizza," he answered quickly.

"Here, take this, boy, and from now on, call me Pierre. I want you to come back see me anytime, Niko, you hear? Just don't come when we're real busy with the crowd at dinner time," Pierre said smiling at him.

"I won't. Gee! Thanks for the pizza, Pierre, see you later," said Niko, stuffing the food in his backpack. "Me and Peco, we're going to eat well tonight," he thought to himself. The boy liked Pierre right away.

Dinner was great in the hideout that night. Pizza, and cookies.

Niko retrieved the marbles from his pocket and watched the flames shining through the glass. The intense cobalt color was truly beautiful. One particular marble was deep blue, almost indigo.

When he twisted the marble in his hand, the flames reflected the indigo color on the wall, dancing on the grooves. It was like the candle reflecting through the church stained glass window. Truly magical!

He looked at his drawing on the wall and as he moved the marble in several directions while looking through them, an idea slowly formed in his head.

"What about if I had colored chalks like those we had in school for drawing? I could mix colors together to blend it on the wall."

He had watched his grandfather many times mixing several colors together to obtain a smooth effect for his Santons.

"That'll work! I've got to get chalks, tomorrow."

The next day after work, Niko went by the store in the village to look for chalks. They came in a package of twenty, every colors he wanted. When he counted his coins, he didn't have enough to buy the chalks.

His heart was crushed. He wanted the chalks so badly to work on his drawing. All day during work on the boat, he had been blending the colors in his head. Niko didn't know what to do.

He hesitated for a moment, looking around the store where several other people looked at different items.

"What if I'd asked the saleslady to let me have the chalks for the amount of money I've got? I'll pay for the difference later?" he wondered.

The saleslady didn't looked too friendly at all. Niko didn't hesitate. He picked up the box of chalks quickly to slide it in one of his pocket. He had to have these chalks no matter what.

"Give me what you just put in your pocket, you little thief, right now," said an angry voice in his ear.

When he heard the man's voice, the boy froze instantly.

CHAPTER EIGHT

Niko's Misery

Niko recognized the voice immediately. He was mortified. Father O' Mally who was also passing through the store, had seen the whole incident with the chalks.

The boy, turned pale, slowly turned around to see Father O' Mally standing there. Shaking like a leaf, he gave him the stolen chalks. The others didn't notice anything unusual in the busy store.

"Go outside, Niko, and wait for me," the young priest told him.

"Why did you steal, Niko. Why didn't you asked me for this?," said the Father angrily when they were outside.

"I'm sorry, Father, I didn't have enough money for the chalks I needed for my work," Niko answered, remorsefully and teary-eyed when seeing the disappointed look on Father O' Mally's face.

"Here, take your package of chalks, it's paid for. Don't let me catch you stealing again, Niko. This is bad. I thought better of you. I've to go now. I'm in a hurry. We'll talk about this later," the Father said leaving the distressed boy on the sidewalk.

On his way back to his hideout, Niko felt ashamed.

He had disappointed his good friend. What in the world came over him to do such a thing? Oppa had taught him the difference between right and wrong.

Crying in his lonely cave, he begged his Blessed Mother to forgive him for his behavior.

"Please, Blessed Mother, forgive Niko for stealing the chalks. I'm heartbroken for what I did and for hurting Father O' Mally," the miserable boy prayed in distress. Niko cried himself to sleep with Peco in his arms.

The faithful little pooch seemed to understand that his master was in pain. Licking his tears, he curled up close to the boy's chest.

A few hours later, both woke up to eat a meager dinner of left over bread and cheese with baked wild onions. The pizza from Pierre was long gone. Niko had made a little oven like, with stones and baked all the vegetables under ashes.

The boy took both lamps close to the wall to work on his drawing. Retrieving the box of colored chalks from his backpack, he went to work. The orphan poured his soul in the drawing of his sunset. Little by little, as he was carefully filling the rugged surface with his chalks, his distress lessened.

It was hard on his small fingers, touching, smoothing, caressing the wall from time to time, until he was satisfied.

The sunset was taking shape as he worked late into the night, and then, he fell asleep again on his bedroll next to Peco. He would only catch a few hours of sleep before dawn.

Niko was used to rising with the sun since he was small. He valued this even more from his hideout. It was his favorite time to see the sunrise over the hill as he listened to the birds in the trees. It gave him a sense of freedom, breathing the fresh air of the wilderness.

Father O' Mally got back to the Presbytery from his meeting feeling tired. He had put a long day of work with poor families. It was always exhausting for him. The letter that he had been waiting for from his sister, Kate, was on his desk. He had written to her the week before to inquire about something.

The matter had bothered him enormously in the past weeks. Hopeful that this would help, he anxiously read Kate's letter. With each line, his heart mellowed toward Niko for what he feared became reality.

Marseille, April, 5, 1952
Dear Paddy
I have done the research you were interested in. I don't know if what I found would help you.
Marius, the famous Santons woodcarver, was one of the best. He was indeed the same person that you meet during our Art Festival in Marseille several years ago.
When I introduced you to him, Marius and I had worked together many times for our Art Shows. He was a quiet, friendly man. Unfortunately, I lost track of him after the Marseille Liberation in 1945.
However, after doing further researches in our archives at the museum, through the latest church records, and by talking to his neighbors, I found the following.
Marius became a recluse following the death of his son, Nicholas and his wife Maria. Both were killed during a liberation battle in an ambush with the Nazis in Marseille.
Afterward, Marius sold all his olive groves at La Madrague, his estate on the east side of Marseille. With the help of his housekeeper, he raised his three years old grandson.
Marius Santini died on March 1ˢᵗ this year. Following his burial a week later, his 10 year old grandson, Niko, the only relative, was sent to an orphanage around Avignon..
I hope this will help you, dear Paddy. Please keep in touch. We all look forward to seeing you at Easter. The twins miss you.

Love,
Your sister Kate

Patrick and Kate were very close, always spending holidays together and keeping in touch. Patrick O' Mally, now in his late twenties, was born and raised in Marseille where he went to school. When he finished college in Aix-en-Provence, he went directly to the Seminary outside Avignon.

Fresh out of the seminary, Patrick was sent to Cassis small congregation of *Sainte-Marie- des-Pêcheurs* church. His sister Kate, two year older, remained in the family home after college.

Both of their parents passed away several years ago. Kate, married, had a pair of twins, and presently worked at the Vieux Marseille museum where she met her husband who was its Curator.

Tall and slender, Father O' Mally had blondish hair and crystal-clear blue eyes, a sign of his Irish ancestry. The young priest was well respected by everyone in the village. He was putting long hours in his busy schedule. He worked closely with the Sisters of the catholic school located next to the church.

His devotion to helping the poor was remarkable. Although his Irish temper flared up once in a while, he loved working with children. He also loved Sport and frequently was seen playing ball with the boys in the courtyard.

Holding Kate's letter in his hand, Father O' Mally was distressed. He reflected on the present situation at hand and what should be his next move.

Niko was, indeed, an orphan.

"Oh, Lord! This little boy must keeps such heavy grief in his heart," he sighted, for he knew how much Niko loved his grandfather. Somehow the young priest had sensed it immediately at their first meeting.

The constant boy's answer, "*he is sleeping*" rang in his mind. The boy didn't lie after all. His grandfather *was* eternally asleep. It now became clear to the Father why Niko was so evasive during their conversations.

"Where does he stay at night. What is his work like? I must find this out. It's no wander the boy sticks to his dog so much. This orphan is all alone," he sighted with anguish. Father prayed a long time for the small boy.

"I must talk to Niko soon and be extra careful with my questions or he will run away again," he decided before retiring that evening.

The following evening, Niko was still upset from the day before. His actions weighted on his heart. He felt gloomy about the disappointment he had caused Father O' Mally.

After cleaning the deck, his day was finally over, he called Gus down below to get his wages. Niko saw his boss's glassy eyes. He knew immediately that it was a mistake to deal with Gus now.

"What's big idea, bothering me like that for your money?" Gus told the boy in a slurred voice, almost felling off the step. "I'll pay you when I'm good and ready, you good for nothing."

I know where you came from, I'm no dummy, I'll report you to the cops if you bother me again, that's what I'll do," Gus continued, threatening the shaking boy, while slapping him hard on the face and pushing him down in the ropes.

"Git going, don't bother me again," he yelled as he stumbled on the deck.

Niko grabbed his pack and ran out of the boat with Peco in his tracks. He sped all the way to the top of the slope, terrified, the hard hit on his face still burning. He had never seen Gus in such a state before.

His loyal pooch was sitting next to him in the dense shrubs, letting out little yaps and licking his hands. From the day he had discovered the short- cut to the cave, which saved him a good mile, Niko had gone that way each time.

Fearful, he didn't dare to go to buy some bread. He was too scared he would run into Gus. His nightly hangout, the *Bar de la Marine,* was not far from the bakery.

Niko couldn't believe Gus rage.

So, he climbed back the steep hill to the hideout, replaying the scene in his head.

It took all his determination to go back to work the next day. He was surprised that Gus didn't mention anything. It was as if the incident never happened. Niko worked silently, tackling the fish cleaning as usual.

"I'm going to the warehouse to take care of business. You make sure you get all your work done when I'm gone, boy," Gus said as he left the boat.

"Boy, he always called me, boy. Never once, he has called me by my name," the boy muttered silently to himself, cleaning his fish load.

The rude man was fine during the day, working hard when the fishermen got back from the sea to unload their catch. His boat rarely leaves the Port.

The fish load was dumped on Gus's boat by mid-morning. Niko cleaned and washed the bloodied fish guts on the deck afterward. It was a messy job. The packing in crates was done by Gus. Then shipping to the warehouse and later to the market by truck.

The boy hadn't forgotten Gus's threat. Far from it. He was too well aware of it. Whenever he thought about it, he started to panic.

What if Gus did call the authorities about me? How did he know about me anyway? Niko knew too well where he would end up.

Chapter Nine

Niko's Kingdom

April brought Spring all through the hills. Sunday after church, Niko didn't see Father O' Mally who was busy with the Passover preparations. He felt a sense of relief for he still was regretful about his past action.

The boy decided to go hiking in the hills with Peco. He wanted to see new territory further uphill. He packed his knapsack with food Pierre had given him the night before and filled his thermos. On the way to the top of the hill, he was overwhelmed with a sense of freedom.

Provencal wildflowers called *"Thumbnails,"* popped out everywhere like a multicolored carpet around him. They were white, pale pink, purple, and some with a blue and red border.

The heavenly aroma of the lavender filled the air along the steep trail. In the background, the celadon trees brought out their vivid touch of green to the landscape. Niko enjoyed seeing the umbrella and Aleppo pines which grew on the limestone acid soil.

Wild or cultivated, the characteristic olives trees were seen everywhere. Filled with happiness, Niko listened to the silence broken only by the chirping birds flying from one tree to another.

When he reached the very top, he sat on the green pine needles. These too were aromatic, as were the fragrant herbs around him. There was not a cloud in the sky.

From where he sat, he could see Cassis down below. It looked like a jewel with fishing boats bobbing on the sea like miniature toys. The coastline shined in the brilliant sun, stretching itself all the way to Marseille with the sea crashing and edging the cliffs with white foam.

It looked exactly like the postcards Niko had seen in some tourists shop. Searching further in the distance, he found what he was looking for. Yes! There it was.

The *Chateau d'If* standing in the sea across Marseille. He had visited the old fortress once when Oppa took him there with the tourist boat.

They had visited the ancient cell, according to Alexander Dumas's novel, where the *Count of Monte Cristo* had been imprisoned for so long, Niko had enjoyed that trip.

He lay down on his back, closing his eyes while remembering that day. He felt a clutch somewhere in his chest. His eyes began to burn. Tears which usually came with Oppa's memory, were ready to spill. "You have to get used to the idea you're alone now," he mumbled wiping his eyes.

He whistled for the wandering pooch to come eat a cheese sandwich. Peco noisily slurped the water given to him and went back to his hunt. "So much to see in this new territory!"

Niko felt at home in this part of the hills, enjoying his freedom in the wild. As he looked around him, he realized he was not as alone as he had thought. Every gully in the windswept hills harbored creatures, big or small.

He remembered that coming back late from work, he had often seen the dark form of animal running swiftly through the undergrowth. Perhaps a weasel or squirrel doing their last hunt before night.

Once, he had seen a possum hanging down from an olive tree a few yards from him. The insolent creature stared at Niko with its beady eyes without moving a muscle. Peco was going wild with barking. The worse of all was when Peco had cornered a skunk.

Niko had hoped to see a fox some day on the hill. His dream was about to come true. It was the cutest little creature he had seen since he came to the hideout. Its pointed red muzzle suddenly pocked out from a bush close to where he sat.

The boy kept very still so as not to frighten him. His shinny round eyes were like tiny black buttons. Oppa had lectured him while camping about the seriousness of touching a cub.

Unless it was injured, it was better not to handle baby animals, for getting them used to human smell was harmful. After a few minutes, the little creature left as fast as it came, probably to catch up with his parents.

The sun was still high in the sky when he saw a red tail eagle soaring above his head.

Niko followed its majestic flight over the hills as far as he could until he lost sight of it.

It was a Bonelli Eagle.

His grandfather had told him about this endangered species, so very protected in the Calanques.

It was then that Niko found the fig tree.

It was crammed with fruits, not yet ripped. Perhaps they would be ready in another month. The old tree grew its knotted branches in every direction, giving it a distinct character. Niko let his finger run over the rough trunk, and liked the feeling. He planned to draw this tree sometime. This old tree would be *his* tree.

The boy lay beneath it, growing lazy, loving this wild hill. When a soft breeze touched his cheek it felt good to him. He watched the silvery leaves on the olive trees below moved by the gentle wind.

"Maybe we could spend the night up here," he thought.

And so they did. It was so peaceful, here. Since his escape, he had learned to identify quickly the sound around him.

He knew which wood to gather for the fire or which food was edible. After the frightful, stormy night of his escape, Niko wasn't afraid of the wild anymore.

The thought of his Father's picture in the cave haunted him still. "Why?" The same question kept rolling through his mind. He had checked the chamber a number of times thoroughly but to no avail.

On several occasions, Niko had wished to confide his adventures and discoveries to Father O' Mally, but this was not possible.

He must keep his escape a secret, specially now.

At sundown he built a fire between rocks in a gully, away from the old fig tree. His grandfather had shown him how to built a fire without smoke. Now Niko had adopted this method during the time that he stayed in the hills.

It didn't have to be at work before noon the next day. He had enough food for the dinner with the left over Pan-bagnat Pierre had given him. He went in search of wild mint to brew tea. The tin-dishes he had found in the cave's chamber were very useful to him now.

From where he stood, the boy became spellbound by the sunset descending on the Mediterranean. He watched the hues gradually melting onto each other.

Soft amethyst turned into flames as if painted by a brush. The orange sun changed slowly to vermilion, to finally shape itself into a great big ball of fire plunging into the sea.

The entire phenomena lasted only a few minutes. Oh! How he wished he could draw this on his wall. He must come back again, bring a drawing pad with his color chalks to capture this enchanted picture. It was far better that seeing the sunset from the cave.

Afterward, Niko lay on a bed of pine needles with his mutt next to him. Peco was exhausted by all his running around through the hill. Niko watched the indigo sky above, studded with thousands of sparkling stars.

Soon the golden moon appeared. He just stared at it, wishing, wondering, what it must be like to live up there.

Since he was an early riser, he had time for himself. He had seen the Old Annie several times too at the market, helping her with her basket. She always filled his pockets with cookies.

Niko knew that he must go back to face Father O' Mally sometime. It was difficult for him to face the good friend he had so badly disappointed.

Lying there, watching the golden moon, he thought about the chalks incident. How could he repair the friendship with the Father again?

The cicadas singing in the balmy night slowly made him drowsy. Soon the boy fell into a deep, peaceful sleep, unaware that the following day a storm would bring painful havoc into his life.

Chapter Ten

The Unleashed Fury

The flaming sun dipped slowly into the sea when Niko, while finishing hosing the deck, stumbled on the ropes behind him by accident. The following sequences of events happened too fast for the boy to control it.

Coming up from below, Gus, who was already far from being sober, got hit by the water from the hose right in the face. As fast as a snake, with his big hands, the man grabbed Niko by the neck to pin him down. Removing his belt with the other hand, he started beating the boy furiously.

"I'm sorry, Gus. It was an accident. I didn't mean it," the boy screamed, trying to protect his face with his arms. But Gus unleashed his fury on the youngster, who was screaming under the searing lashes.

"What d' you mean, you didn't mean it, you good for nothing. I told you before, I'll teach you to be more careful," he yelled still beating on Niko.

Peco, waiting on the pier for his master, reacted to his screams, leaped on board immediately and bit Gus in the ankle. The man lost his balance, let go of Niko, and fell flat on his face, swearing at the dog.

Niko seized this chance to jump off the boat. Barefoot and lumping on one foot, he ran as best he could to the end of the pier, made a turn and headed right for the church.

His body hurt as he entered the side door, and fell on the floor at the feet of his Blessed Mother. Crouched in the dark, he cried for help.

"Dear blessed mother, please help Niko. I hurt so much," he sobbed faintly.

As Father O' Mally was closing the church for the night, he saw a form lying by the statue. He approached closer and in the flicker of the statue's candle, he recognized the silver medallion around Niko's neck. The waif crouched like a small, wounded bird, wept at the statue's feet.

The priest went down on his knees but the second he touched him, the boy screamed, obviously in great pain.

"God! Niko, what on earth happened. Who did this to you?" he asked the speechless boy.

"Come, let me look at you. Where does it hurt?" He could see the boy was in great pain as he tried to stand up to follow him. Who would be so cruel to hurt a small boy this way?" he sighted, furiously.

He called Sister Anne to help him take Niko to the school infirmary. Both were astonished to see the red marks on his neck.

Seeing the blood on his shirt, the Father fell his Irish temper rise inside.

The Sisters who helped in the hospital from time to time knew how to take care of the semi-conscious boy. After undressing him, they were shocked at the ugly lash marks on his back.

With great care, they washed Niko before putting ointment over the sores and then put him to bed. Exhausted, he fell asleep almost instantly. Peco refused to leave the room and lay at his feet.

"What happened. Why is Niko in such a state?" Father O' Mally wondered. His clothes reeked of fish smell. The Father had seen kids working on the old port, off and on. Working with the poor, he had seen beaten kids before but not to this extent.

"Perhaps Niko worked in the port too. But why the beating? Who would do such a thing?" He had no answers and had to wait until the boy could tell him.

He mulled over this for a long time, sitting by Niko's bed side and checking on him often. He had been feeding the pooch, who wouldn't leave the boy no matter what.

Niko called a name several times in his sleep. Father O' Mally thought he heard a name like "Oppa." He would have to talk with Niko soon. The boy needed to be cared for. The young priest knew he would have to approach this waif carefully. He knew the boy too well.

After reading Kate's letter, it didn't take Father O' Mally long to add two. It was most likely that Niko had escaped during his transfer to the orphanage. He was the type of kid who could do this.

But the Father hadn't heard no report of the escape. Why?

Was it possible that the Orphanage didn't report this?

No matter how he turned the questions in his head, he had no answers. Father knew about an Orphanage located several miles outside of Avignon. In any case, something would have to be done about Niko.

During the night, Niko woke up, a little out of sorts to found himself in a bed. His entire body was on fire. The Sisters had given him a tisane to drink to help him relax, but when he turned on his back he couldn't sleep. Switching to lay on his stomach, he finally went to sleep.

It was past noon the next day when Niko, still disoriented woke up. Laying on the rug below the bed, Peco went to him instantly to lick his hand and whined a bit to let him know he was there.

He got up with difficulty, noticed clean clothes on a chair, and then remembered what happened. It was painful to get dressed. The tennis shoes next to his clothes were not his.

Niko walked painfully to the door of a hallway, hearing the Sisters preparing lunch in the school's cafeteria. The Father who was helping them, saw him.

"Niko, how you're doing my boy? Do you feel like eating, yet?" he asked the limping boy.

"Hello, Father! Thank you for helping me, I feel better now. Maybe I should go home," the boy said, not looking the priest in the eyes.

"I don't think you should move too much yet. You've had quite a bad time," the Father said.

Niko didn't answered. He knew that he should not stay too long here. Somehow, he must get back to the cave, but he could hardly move.

"I do feel tired yet, Father. Perhaps I should rest some more," he said.

"Good! Then come sit and have some lunch with me. Then you can rest some more this afternoon. Tonight, will be soon enough to decide," Father O' Mally said taking him gently to a table.

"The good Sisters have lunch for us. You need to get your strength back."

"Tell me, Niko, are the people where you work mean to you?"

Niko remained silent, eating his cheese sandwich, but Father O' Mally saw him clinch his fist.

"Niko, I am your friend. You must trust me. You know that I don't mean any harm to you. I am very concerned about you and I want to help if you're in trouble."

"I had an accident at work when I stumbled in the ropes," he finally told Father.

"Has the person you work for done this to you?"

"Ya! But he didn't mean it," he quickly answered.

"Where do you work, Niko,"

"There it is! I knew that was coming. Now what do I do?" the boy thought staying on his guard.

"I can't tell you Father or he will hurt you, too."

"I can take care of myself, my boy, don't worry about me. Why do you have to work anyway? What about school, Niko? We have a great school here, and we can take care of you," the Father ventured.

"I have to work, Father, I have to. I don't have time for school now."

"What about your grandfather? What does he say about this working?"

Before he had finished the question, Father O' Mally knew immediately he had pushed too far.

Niko instantly went back inside his shell.

"That's OK, Niko. We'll talk more another time. I'll come to see you tonight when I come back, I must go do some work in the village right now," he said getting up from the table.

It was enough for today. He wouldn't get any more information, he thought. Niko walked back to the room, his whole body sore. He knew he must rest, but at the same time, he knew he must leave.

Before departing for the village, the Father gave instruction to the Sisters to let Niko sleep. The boy did need rest for sure. Maybe tomorrow he could talk with him again.

Before dinner time, Sister Anne came to change his bandages and brought Niko some soup and a fruit on a tray. Niko thanked her and told her he would sleep again for he felt tired.

After she had closed the door, he ate the soup and saved the fruit for later. At nightfall, Niko got dressed again, motioning to Peco to be quiet. They both left silently while the Sisters were at evening prayers. The waif hoped to reach the slope which was behind the church without been seen by anyone.

He grabbed a sturdy stick to start the hard climb, stopping often for his entire body hurt. It took him a long time in slow motion, before he finally reached the hideout.

He tried to lay on his bedroll but he hurt too much to sleep. The lonely boy cried for a long time, wishing Oppa would be here. His grandfather would know what to do for him with his healing herbs.

His eyes strayed to the long wall at the end of the cave, straining to see his drawings. Tonight, he couldn't do this. Maybe tomorrow.

If only he could sleep. It was at that moment that Niko realized that he didn't have his backpack.

When he ran from the boat, he had left without it. He had a bit of money left, but worst of all, most precious of all, his parents picture was inside.

Everyday when coming to work, Niko hid his backpack in a deep corner of the boat where he knew Gus couldn't see it. Now, he trembled at the thought of Gus finding it. Would he?

Chapter Eleven

The Chase

Fatigued by a long day of work in the village, Father O' Mally wanted to see how Niko was getting along. He found the empty bed with the note on the pillow.

Thank You, Father and the Sisters for helping Niko. Me and Peco must leave now. Please, don't worry about us. We're fine. Niko

"I did pushed too much, I failed the boy! Now what?" he sighted, discouraged. He couldn't believe the endurance of Niko.

This streetwise urchin from Marseille who could hardly walk this morning, certainly had grits. Was he in the streets?

The Father had figured the situation out after Kate's letter. There were hundreds of kids like Niko in the big city living on their own.

He had seen them, worked with them, but this was the little village of Cassis, not Marseille.

"If only I knew where he worked in the village. Father O' Mally felt responsible for the boy.

Niko was worn out by pains, fatigue, and weakness. The long climb had diminished his strength. He finally went back to sleep until late the next afternoon.

He ate the banana that Sister Anne gave him for his dinner yesterday. It was quite an effort to light a fire to brew chamomile tea. Oppa used to give this when he was sick. He had trouble using his arms and his right leg made him limp.

Niko didn't know what he would do next. He was too weak to go down the boat yet, but he worried about his backpack. He would have to go at night for sure when Gus was gone to the bar.

There was no way he could go back to work there anyway. Maybe he should talk with Father O' Mally after all, or maybe Pierre could help him?

He didn't know what to do.

How was he going to survive without food or money?

He dragged himself outside to sit in the sun on his favorite log and watched the sea in the distance. He was lost without his backpack.

It took all his strength to make a soup with the wild carrots and onions he had saved in the cave.

Sleeping on his back was most difficult. It was several days before he could sleep comfortably. He had enough wood around the cave to make a fire but he miss bread terribly.

Little by little, Niko started to feel more like himself. He walked up to his fig tree to exercise his leg. He loved to spend time there, just sitting watching the sea below, drawing the ever changing sunset on his pad.

It was on his way down that he discovered the spring, probably coming from Mont Puget down the hill like hundreds of other springs. His surprise was even greater when he saw fish running down stream.

This would help him survive once he found a way to catch them. He remembered then how Oppa had shown him once during their camping how to fish without a fishing pole. He had carved a spear made out of bamboo stick, and with patience had speared a fish for their dinner.

"Why not give it a try?" the boy thought.

Niko searched for the right reed to shape carefully with his knife in order to form an arrow, remembering his grandfather's instructions. It took many tries and with all his patience to finally spear a good-sized trout.

He and Peco could now eat something more substantial with his fennel and wild carrots. Peco would sure go for that too.

Bringing their dinner back to the hideout, Niko's spirit soared after he had cooked the delicious trout over the fire. "What luck to find that spring," the boy thought to himself.

Days went by before Niko thought to go in the village to try to fetch his backpack on the boat. Perhaps, he also could go to see Pierre.

During his time in the hideout, Niko had found out that it was difficult to draw in the cave during the day. When the sunlight was hitting the wall, it distorted the lighting inside. It was only after sundown that he was able to work.

The five-gallon container of oil for the lamps that he had found in the chamber was great. This was his best light for working at night. Since the beating, he had trouble lifting his right arm, but he kept working at it, moving it all around from time to time.

Finally one evening, he decided to work on his drawing, which was coming along slowly. Since he had the chalks, he had corrected his colors in a smoother way to obtain a similar effect he had seen in the sunset from up on the hill.

After working with it for a while, Niko was satisfied but he knew that he needed more guidance with his art. Perhaps he should go to "The Artisan" and look at some art books to get some ideas about it.

More than a week went by before Niko felt that he could go down the trail to the village. The limp on his right leg was lessening due to several walks up the hill. He was extra careful not to run into Father O' Mally or Gus and went through the alley to see Pierre.

"Niko, my boy! Where have you been? I kept some food for you the other day. I was worried about you."

"I've been sick, Pierre, but I'm better now. Gee! thanks Chef!" He kept calling him Chef, because it sounded better. Pierre had a bag in his hand for him.

"Where his your backpack? I want to stuff this in," he told the boy.

" I left it at work the other day. I'm going there now to get it," he said quickly.

"Well! Here! It's a surprise, Niko, for you and your grandfather," Pierre said, knowing well that there was no grandfather.

"Thanks, Pierre, I'm sure I'll like that. I've got to go now. Bye!"

Pierre watched the boy leave, noticing the limping.

"Good grief! What happened to that boy? He sure looks pale," he questioned himself, wondering where this waif spends his nights.

On his way from "The Ratatouille" Niko went by the book shop to look through the art book and get ideas for his sunset. He had been here several times before but knew that Raoul, the owner, hated to see him in his shop.

"Better slipped in by the back door" he thought to himself.

"Watch this, Peco," he told the pooch as he put his package on the ground before entering the shop.

"The Artisan" swarmed with people looking through the bookshelves. Raoul had his eyes immediately on the ragged boy looking through the rows of books.

Niko found what he was looking for in an art book on painting by the great masters. It was the sunset of his dream, right there in front of his eyes.

Since he didn't have the money to buy such a book, maybe he could just borrow it and bring it back later. He just could see himself blending theses colors on his wall. Raoul turned once more to look at Niko, before stepping into the back room to get something for a client.

The temptation was too much. Swiftly, his small hands stuffed the book in his shirt. Sneaking rapidly between people, he made his escape through the back door, picked up Pierre's package, and ran.

His heart beat stopped when the door alarm buzzed.

"Come here. Stop, you, thief," yelled, Raoul, furiously running behind him in the street.

Niko flew like the wind without stopping, all the way to the end of the street.

He heard the police whistle in the distance. Surely they'd catch him this time. He was certain of it.

"Please, let me get to the slope!" he begged as he reached the street's corner out of breath. He knew that he if he could get to the slope, it would be difficult for his pursuers to see him as he hid himself in the garrigue.

He was breathless as he got to the trail, dragging his legs, wanting to scream with pain. Sensing the imminent danger, Peco sped along in his tracks. The boy hoped that no one was behind him, listening as he started to climb to the cave. Closer to the hideout, his instincts told him not to stop there but to continue all the way to the fig tree.

A few minutes later, he thought that he heard voices in the distances.

"Was it the wind or did his pursuers find his tracks? Or was his mind playing tricks?"

Holding the trunk with both hands, he climbed his favorite tree with Peco. The branches were so heavy that he could lay on them and stay out of sight. He decided to remain there until he was sure that it was safe for him to go back to the hideout.

It took a long while for his heartbeat to calm down.

"They must've given up the chase," he thought, hopeful that the way was cleared. Being used to the silence of the hills, he listened intently for any strange noise. It was late when Niko and Peco went back down to the hideout.

The boy piled the bushy branches behind them to cover the entrance and before lighting his lamps. He retrieved the book from his sweat soaked shirt to put it on the bed with great care. He would return it later, he was sure of this, but first he must study it.

He was starved. It was then, that Niko remembered Pierre's package left by the entrance of the hideout.

To his surprise when he opened it, all kinds of goodies filled the bag.

There was broiled chicken, baked ratatouille in a jar, and a big piece of cake with a note at the bottom of the bag.

"For, Niko, the best little helper in town."

Although it was late at night, both the boy and the dog ate a great deal, with lots left over for tomorrow. After the meal, Niko washed his hands and with excitement, opened the book. It was an expensive book. He knew that right away.

Bringing his lamps closer, he studied each page religiously, avidly. Extraordinary paintings in brilliant colors came alive in front of his eyes. Works of art of the masters filled the pages with paintings that Niko had never seen before. He looked at each one in wonder.

Van Gogh, Monet, Cezanne, Gauguin, Dufy, all there on these pages for him to learn their techniques.

Niko was fascinated by the smoothness of colors melting into each other so well. He savored the magnificent paintings, page after page, until one of them held his attention. It was the sunset he had seen in the store. The sunset of his dream.

"It's exactly what I need to finish my sunset, Peco," he told the pooch, already snoring at his feet. The poor little mutt was exhausted.

The boy took his light, approached the wall to work on his drawing. His fingers worked with the chalks with great care, blending the colors as in the picture. His physical pain diminished, soothing his misery.

Slowly under his touch, the curving grooves formed the indigo ocean bathed by a glowing sunset similar to what he had seen from the fig tree.

He was unaware that tears streamed his face as he poured his heartache into the drawing with every stroke.

When early dawn peeked through the sky, Niko couldn't stand any longer. Exhausted, he fell on his bedroll, totally spend.

Niko didn't know that he had just created the drawing which would turn his life around.

CHAPTER TWELVE

Trapped

Spring 1952

Easter went by and permitted Father O' Mally to enjoy a few well-earned vacation days with Kate and her family in Marseille. A retired priest from a village near by took over his duties.

On the evening of his return home, he learned about the incident at "The Artisan" from two policemen at his door asking questions. Would a small boy in his parish fit the description they gave him?

He was deeply dismayed for he immediately thought of Niko.

What in the world was happening with the boy?

Was this rebellion from his part after the beating?

He understood the boy's loneliness and insecurity after the terrible ordeal of having been abused. It just didn't make any sense. He must look for the boy quickly before the police find him, but where?

After taking care of his imminent duty the following evening, he went to search for Niko. He checked all over the village, on the marketplace, in the streets, but to no avail.

He was sure that the homeless boy went into hiding, but where would he go? He had no friend and certainly no family to go to. Did he run away from Cassis?

"Niko is a lonely soul living from day to day," he thought. He was desperate.

He had hoped that the boy would come to him, and it was getting very late when he gave up the search. Perhaps, tomorrow evening I should go look around in the old port. The night of the beating he smelled of fish. Was he working on a boat?"

Meanwhile, quite accidentally, Niko made a strange discovery in the back chamber. The heavy cardboard case he had placed under the spring with a pan on top to catch water, suddenly got him curious.

When he checked it, he realized that it was becoming wet. He had paid no attention to it since he slid it there. At the time he thought that it was a case of ammunition.

The spring dripped into the pan slowly but at least he had water to cook and to drink. That night when he got water from the pan, he saw that the cardboard case was tearing in one corner showing something inside.

To his surprise after opening the case, he found small packages sealed in plastic containing different things. Some package were dried food mostly. In another package, he found an emergency kit with bandages and a little sewing kit.

After his trouble with Raoul, he didn't dare go down to the village for food for fear of being caught. He worried about his backpack still on the boat. If Gus got a hold of it this would be disastrous.

Niko was thankful for the contents of the cardboard case, which would come in handy. His Blessed Mother once more came to his rescue. First with the spring, then with this. His flight through the hills after the chase from "The Artisan" had taking its toll. He was still pretty weak and slept a lot during the day.

A few days later. the boy decided to go and, no matter what, to retrieve his pack. The trick was to reach the boat after dark when Gus had gone to his favorite hangout in town. Waiting for sundown he went down the trail watching his every move, careful not to be seen.

He was sneaking closer to the boat, checking for light inside, when a thought hit him.

"What if Gus hired someone to work in my place? What if that someone was aboard?"

He waited a few minutes but still saw no light shining inside the boat. Everything was quiet. He knew where his backpack was. All he needed to do was to grab it quickly and scram.

Once he made up his mind, he motioned to Peco to sit tight on the pier and wait for him. Niko jumped on the deck. Then, heart in his throat, he tiptoed to where his pack was stashed and grabbed it quickly. He let his breath out. It was still in the same place. Gus hadn't touched it.

At the same time, Father O' Mally, snooping around the old port, happened to notice Peco sitting there. If the dog was there, surely, so was the boy.

Afraid that Peco, who knew him well, would bark at his approach, he went silently behind a tree and waited.

Sure enough, Niko jumped out of the boat, whistling for the pooch, before he ran all the way to the corner of the street close to the church. Careful not to be seen, the priest followed them at a distance, thinking that Niko was on his way to see him until they went behind the church.

From there, the boy climbed a slope to continue on up the hill.

"Where in the world were they going?" thought the Father.

The trail they took was quite steep. He wasn't familiar with it. He listened to the boy talking to Peco along the way.

The path became very dense, and his cassock kept catching in the bushes. Keeping behind at a safe distance, he barely could see the boy. He had no idea where the trail was leading in this wilderness, but the boy surely knew where he was going in the dark.

"This is typical of Niko," he thought, relieved to have found him. After a while, Niko slowed down, stopped to remove a large bush from something, and then slipped through a hole, followed by Peco.

The boy replaced the bush from the inside. Father O' Mally waited a few minutes before approaching quietly in case the dog would give the alert.

Barely noticeable, a dim light appeared through the bush.

"So! That's the secret place, a cave," he sighted, wondering how to approach the lad. After a few seconds he removed the bush silently before stepping through, taking Niko by surprise. Peco immediately came to smell his hands, yapping in joy to see him.

Niko stood speechless. He was trapped.

"You're in deep trouble, Niko! The police are searching everywhere in the village for you. Unless you come back with me tonight, you will end up in reform school."

The Father emphasized to him the seriousness of his actions.

Niko couldn't find his voice at first but finally answered the Father.

"I'm sorry, Father! I know you're mad at me," he finally articulated with great difficulty.

"Sorry won't cut it, Niko. You've done great wrong this time. Why? What in the world had gotten into you?"

"You see, Father, I just borrowed the book. I needed it to study the colors for my drawing," the boy said, pointing at the wall with his finger.

Turning around, Father O' Mally followed the boy's gesture toward the wall, then, he moved closer, truly astonished by what he saw on the limestone.

The golden sunset over the cobalt sea with seagulls swooping above it mystified him. It was incredibly beautiful.

"You did this, Niko? How can you draw so well without schooling?"

the priest marveled.

"I've been drawing since grandfather showed me when I was just a little tike. This is what I like to do best, Father. It's why I come here to hide in my secret place, to draw. Niko don't feel so lonely that way," the homeless boy told him, holding back tears.

"You're under my protection, now, Niko. Nobody will hurt you anymore, I'll see to that," the young priest said, mellowing at the sight of the waif.

"The police will put me in an orphanage. I don't want to go to an orphanage. That's why I ran away before," Niko said, letting tears spill at last.

His small shoulders shook as he sobbed.

"First thing tomorrow, we'll give the book back. I'll talk to the police, to repair the damages you've done. You'll be under the protection of the church from now on. They'll listen to me," Father O' Mally affirmed, while hugging him.

He went to take another look at the drawing. This was unbelievable.

"How could he have created this in such a poor state of health?" he was puzzled. He could see that the boy was still limping. He looked around the cave to look at Niko's quarters.

The young priest was wondering how this boy had managed to stay here for so long, let alone to climb the trail when he was in such a bad state. This kid had guts for sure.

He watched Niko gathering his meager belongings to go. He had organized his hiding place with a wooden case for table next to a bedroll. His clothes were neatly folded on logs. The color chalks were on the ground by the wall.

Everything the boy had stolen was for his art.

Before they stepped out on the trail, Niko took great care that the bush was firmly in place before the entrance. This was his secret place.

Father O' Mally's heart went to Niko as they both headed down the trail, reaching the back of the church in silence with Peco trailing behind them. The Father was troubled by the drawing in the hideout.

"How lonely that little boy must've been to create such a piece of work. Something good must come out of this."

He fed both the boy and the dog before putting them to bed for the night, pleading with Niko to listen and stay put.

For a long time he was deep in thought, praying for the boy's welfare.

Later Father O' Mally came to the decision to call his long time friend.

"Hello Roger, it's Paddy. I need you, my friend. I need to talk to you about something which disturbs me greatly. Could you meet me for lunch tomorrow?" he asked, relieved to finally be sharing his problem with someone.

CHAPTER THIRTEEN

Sunset Over The Sea

May-June, 1952

Roget Gallet and Patrick O' Mally had been close friends since childhood. Both had grown up in Marseille, gone to the same school, and lived in the same neighborhood.

When they went to college in Aix-en-Provence, they became roommates. After college, Paddy studied theology while Roger chose fine arts. They had remained friends all these years.

"What's the matter with Paddy? He sound so worried, I hope that nothing is wrong," thought Roger as he rushed over to the church to meet his friend.

In the school cafeteria, over lunch prepared by the Sisters, Father O' Mally recounted Niko's story.

He told Roger about "The Artisan" incident, motioning toward the orphan, who was eating a few feet away. He never mentioned the boy's drawing.

"I have to make a decision about the boy very quickly before the police takes over the matter. But first, there is something that you must see. This is why I called you, Roger," he told his friend before taking him up the uphill hike.

"Where are you taking me anyway, Paddy?" the man said after climbing some distance.

"Foighme, cara." We're almost there! The Father told Roger, getting back to his native Irish. Besides, the climb will do you good, Roger," he said grinning.

When Roger saw his friend slow down and then remove a bush from a hole, he became curious. They both stooped before entering the cave. Father O' Mally picked up one of the lamp on the floor before lighting it. Then, he took his friend to the wall.

"Have you ever seen anything like this, Roger?" he asked watching his friend's reaction.

Roger remained silent for a few seconds while studying the drawing on the wall. Touching the grooves with his fingers, he stepped backward, then forward to touch it again.

"No, Paddy, I've never seen anything like this," he finally answered in a slow voice. "You're telling me that a ten years old kid created this?"

"The same kid that you saw in the cafeteria a while ago," the Father said, smiling.

Roger had seen Niko briefly at lunch eating at the next table. Father O' Mally had given strict orders to the Sisters not to let him out of their sight when they were gone.

Roger's face was serious as he studied the drawing again.

"This is powerful, Paddy. I read a lot of sadness, loneliness in it. It's hard to believe that a boy that age can feel so much pain. Drawings reveal an artist's state of mind. This one has me totally baffled.

Such a talent must be cultivated. When could I evaluate the boy?" he continued with excitement in his voice.

Going back downhill, the Father recounted Niko's background to his friend.

"I still don't have all the answers about Niko, Roger. The boy keeps a lot to himself and doesn't want to open up yet. This is why I'm so concerned," he told him.

Roger, who didn't have any children, was moved. After the death of his wife, Monique, to leukemia several years ago, he had found solace in his own art.

They both decided to bring Niko to the studio the following afternoon so Roger could evaluate the boy's artistic talent.

The "Roger Gallet Studio" was well known in Cassis. People came to see its watercolor collection from all over the country.

Roger had worked with emotionally needy children before in some art classes he conducted. The drawing on the limestone wall had made a deep impression on him. Drawing on stone was difficult, least of all for a child. He was amazed at the boy's creativity and achievement.

Father O' Mally was somewhat comforted, knowing that his friend would mentor the orphan. Niko deserved some type of happiness in his childhood.

"Now, Niko, just sit right here on that stool in front of the easel," Roger told the boy the next day, placing a tray of pastels in front of him.

"I like you to draw anything that comes to your mind, anything," he told him, standing with Father O' Mally behind the boy.

He watched the youngster's every move. First, the boy touched the pastels, looking at them reverently, almost lovingly. He closed his eyes for a few seconds before his small fingers went quickly to work. It was almost magical to see the boy work.

Niko chose a cobalt color that he mixed carefully with a bit of aqua. He added white before smoothing it with two fingers. He went over this several times until he was satisfied. Afterward, he drew seagulls swooping over the water. He worked swiftly with the pastels.

It was clear to Roger that the boy was right in his element. His eyes shone as he worked in silence. He had totally forgotten both men who sat behind him. Flabbergasted, Roger held his breath, watching the boy concentrate on his work.

"This is very good, Niko. Where did you learn this technique? Roger asked putting his hands on the boy's shoulders.

"I watched, Oppa, many times when he painted his Santons. He always blended his colors like that," he answered.

This was the first time that he had mentioned his grandfather by his nickname in front of anyone since his escape.

Father O' Mally heart squeezed at the boy's revelation, for he knew how much Niko loved his grandfather. He had heard the boy calling Oppa in his dream the night of the beating.

"How would you like to study art with me, Niko?" asked Roger, excited by this little genius.

"I don't have any money for lessons. I'll have to find work first before I could do that," Niko answered quickly.

"Why don't you let me be the judge of that. You have a gift, Niko. It must be cultivated. I'd love to teach you all about art," he said. I'm sure that we could come to some arrangement," Roger continued, grinning at the Father, waiting for comments on his part.

"I must get going to the village, I've work to do there. Let's talk about this tonight over supper when I come back. Besides, Niko has to promise to make a lot of changes in his life," he answered, wanting to make an impression on the orphan.

Niko felt comfortable with Roger right away. They both had a lot in common.

"He loves art too, just like me," the orphan thought.

Both friends discussed Niko's fate for a long time that night, weighting the good and bad options. Decisions had to be made quickly before the authorities took over.

Should Father O' Mally turn the orphan over to the police?

They both decided not to approach Gus, as much as they wanted to. The man needed a good lesson, but in the end, he could make trouble for Niko. They finally decided to send the orphan at the villa to stay with Roger until further decisions were made.

Roger would go to Marseille to apply for the papers necessary to stand as guardian for Niko. The next day, the judge in Marseille explained to Roger in detail that his guardianship would valid until the orphan could be adopted by a family.

Meanwhile, he must take charge of the boy's welfare and see to his education. In a few weeks, school would be out for the summer. It was no use to send Niko there now.

Roger could help him with private lessons to prepare him for school in the fall and work with him in art classes.

The admiration between Roger and Niko was mutual. Since the death of his grandfather, the boy had endured more than his share of turmoil, but he had courage and perseverance for a better future. Roger was sure of this.

Roger's villa, overlooking the Mediterranean on the east side of Cassis, was built in a Provencial style. It was spacious with plenty of room. Niko's life had now changed for the best, with new clothes to wear and his own bedroom. As for Peco, he had never had it so good.

Roger's housemaid, Norma, had a tendency to spoil both of them behind Roger's back. She was a lot like Fifi.

Although his missed life in the hideout from time to time, Niko felt a great respect for his guardian. Every morning he had two hours of schoolwork and art classes in the afternoon. The rest of the time he could have for himself.

Nothing surpassed the art classes where he did what he loved the most, drawing. Roger taught him the different drawing techniques, stimulated by his obvious ability. Niko put all his heart into it. The sunset in the cave had revealed to Roger the deep pain inside the boy.

Roger loved sailing. He was like a different man at the helm of his boat. He sailed the coastal waters, his face to the wind, truly relaxed on the sea, enjoying his weekends on the *"Monique,"* named after his late wife.

The day that he took Niko sailing, the adventurous boy loved it immediately, feeling the sailboat slice through the turquoise sea.

He listened to the sail flapping in the breeze, watching Roger's every move.

"You're going to experience a sun set like you never saw before, Niko," explained Roger.

Weather on the water or hiking in the hills, they enjoyed being with each other. Roger taught him to see everything with his five senses.

"Try to absorb what nature and the sea tells you, Niko. Colors have many languages. Incorporate this into your drawing to reflect their meaning in your own way," he told him.

During the month of June they took several camping trips in the Calanques and the hideout where they stayed at night. Niko took Roger uphill and was proud to show him his fig tree. They went to the spring to catch a few trout for their dinner.

Niko's medallion around his neck had puzzled Roger from the start. Paddy and he had questioned the boy about it once before. When Niko remained silent, they decided better not to push him any further, until that one afternoon when Niko recounted his escape to them. They both trembled as they listened to the boy.

He had never revealed what he had found in the cave chamber or showed the picture of his father and his beautiful mother to anyone.

On their first night in the hideout, Niko finally confided to Roger about the secret of the second chamber. With tears in his eyes the boy, touching his medallion, showed him the picture from his backpack, before taking him through the opening in the wall.

He showed Roger the picture in the crumpled old newspaper. Roger remained silent while reading the article, comparing both pictures and listening to Niko.

"I don't understand any of this. Why is my father's picture in this old newspaper?" Niko asked Roger with tears spilling on his cheeks. Roger went down on his knees holding the boy's shoulders.

"I don't know either, Niko, I can't read this language, but I promise you that I will do everything possible to find out. Will you trust me?" he asked.

"Yes, I trust you, Roger," he answered wiping his tears with his shirt, while Roger looked around the chamber, checking several things on the floor. He understood what he was looking at but decided to keep quiet.

"I never knew my father. If I did, I don't remember him, only what Oppa told me long time ago when I was little," the boy continued.

"What did Oppa told you, Niko?" asked Roger.

"That my parents were both killed during the war when I was just a baby. I wish I could remember them," the boy continue, full of sadness.

"Don't think about it anymore, Niko. For now, let's enjoy our camping here together," he said, hoping to lift the boy's spirits.

In fact, Roger could read the article. He had concluded immediately why those things were there in the chamber. Paddy and he, familiar with the Marseille's liberation, would come up with some explanation.

During the summer vacation, a strong bond grew between the man and the boy. Their times spend together healed both of their wounds. The summer continued to run smoothly. Unfortunately, happiness often has its price for the Fall wind brought sadness to the villa.

Once more, Niko's life would be in the hands of fate.

CHAPTER FOURTEEN

The Changing Winds

June-September, 1952

"Today is June 15. It's your birthday! Niko. I have a surprise for you," Roger told the boy the following Sunday morning.

"We're going to a place that I think you'll like," he told the speechless boy, who had totally forgotten about his birthday.

"Today, I am 11 years old."

Roger had found out Niko's age when filing for his guardianship. They sailed *"The Monique"* to Cap Morgiou, near Cassis.

"Grotte Cosquer" was the famous underwater cave discovered by Henry Cosquer, a Cassis diver. Scientists had proven the authenticity of the drawings found on the walls. Images of seals, penguins, and fish could be dated approximately back to 17,000 BC.

The hand print drawings were much older, from about 27,000 BC. To think that cavemen could draw so well was beyond belief. Niko listened to the guide directing the tour, absorbing each detail like a sponge.

He found out that the Corniche des Cretes in the limestone cliffs of Calanques were some of the highest in France, over 1200 ft, created by the waves forming them during the flooding cycle, and by the glaciers, over the course of the past two million years.

The trip to the grotto was a real treat for Niko, who was asking hundreds of questions. The drawings on the limestone were done with red, yellow, brown and black dyes made out with crushed minerals and fish shell.

The people of Provence always have an excuse to hold a festival. During the summer, festivals are common everywhere, bringing many tourists to Cassis and the villages surroundings. There are folkloric dances everywhere, out door concerts, and, of course, the lavender harvest.

The purple hills are covered with lavender, filling the air with the fragrant scent. The lavender essence, made into perfume, is a great part of the agriculture in Provence.

Most of its picking is done by machine, although in certain areas, as Niko found out, this is still done by hand. On July 15, Cassis celebrated its lavender festival, always a great event all throughout the village.

During the summer months, Roger had to attend several meetings at art galleries all around Provence.

He took Niko along with him so the boy could become familiar with the world famous paintings such as; *Matisse, Duffy, Gauguin, Van Gogh, Cezanne* and many more.

They also visited the medieval castle of Cassis, located on the hilltop above the village. The castle was built in 1381. Roger told Niko that during the One hundred Year Old War, brigands devastated Provence.

Later on, the problem continued with Pirates who hid in the Callanques. Niko wondered if they hid in his cave, too.

Roger and the boy enjoyed going to the market together. It was during one of their trip that Niko bumped into Old Annie again and helped her with her load. Afterward, he also introduced Pierre to Roger.

The Chef was happy to see the boy again. He had worried about him after he had heard what happened in *"The Artisan."* Somehow Pierre knew that this boy was involved in the incident, and he had hoped to see Niko again.

He could see the change in the urchin immediately.

He invited both Roger and Niko to stay for lunch at *"The Ratatouille."*

He was thankful to Roger for taking the orphan boy in, talking a lot about Niko when he went off to walk Peco.

As summer came to an end, the hills turned to brilliant hues. It was time for the grape harvest. During the first week of September, Cassis celebrated its Wine Festival. It was a great event for locals and the tourists coming from the nearby towns. Wine growers tried to outsell each other's product during the festival.

Pierre was busy at the restaurant during that time.

Roger took the boy often for Pan Bagnat lunch, enjoying the Chef's conversation on the terrace.

Niko enjoyed the garden at the villa most of all. It was there, after his afternoon art class, that he spent most of his time, drawing and looking at the sea. Above all, he loved the gazebo.

Roger had it built for Monique a long time ago and herself spent a lot of time there reading. He had planted hybrid roses around it, cultivating them with great care in her memory.

After sailing, this was his second hobby. He took care great pride in his Tea-Roses garden, working there whenever he could, while Niko worked on his drawing inside the gazebo.

Mid-September, Niko entered third grade at the Catholic school in Cassis. The sisters who knew him well were surprised at his progress. Roger's work to prepare him for school had paid off.

The young boy was actually eager to learn and had no trouble following the other students. He had surpassed Roger's expectation in art. Father O' Mally saw Niko often at school, delighted to see the change in him. Roger was doing great work as his guardian.

Patrick O' Mally could see the positive change also in his friend, Roger, for he had seen him at his lowest after the death of Monique.

Life at the villa ran smoothly during fall. Niko grew taller, putting some weight on his skinny frame, while Peco grew fatter by the week.

Norma had a lot to do with this.

All the goodies behind Roger's back, and the good life at the villa had changed both, the boy and the pooch.

The judge in Marseille had checked on Niko's welfare several times and was satisfied. On October 15, Roger received a letter from him, requesting him to come to his office as soon as possible. The judge had a matter of urgency to discuss with him regarding Niko.

Roger anticipated this had to do with the guardianship. The meeting, however, overtook his recent happiness with sadness. He stopped to see Paddy on the way back to inform him of what happened.

The minute that he saw his face, Father O' Mally knew that something was wrong. His friend was pale and could hardly talk.

"What's wrong, Roger, sit down,?" he asked putting his hands on his shoulders.

"I just had a meeting with the judge concerning Niko. The news is not good, Paddy," he managed to tell his friend.

"I must take Niko back to Marseille. There is a family who wants to see him. They're interested in adopting him. What am I going to do, Paddy? Niko is important to me now," he finally let out.

"You knew that this would happen, sooner or later, Roger. The guardianship was only temporary. If you remember, the judge was firm about this from the start," reminded Patrick.

"I know, Paddy, I didn't think it would be so soon, that's all. Niko and I are just getting used to each other. We're doing so many things together.

Why now?" he managed to say with moist eyes.

"Well now, let's analyze the problem together. When are you supposed to take Niko to Marseille?" asked Father O' Mally," troubled as well by this news. Good God!, his friend was falling apart once more.

"The family wants to meet Niko on November 3. I must take him out of school to prepare him for this news."

"How will I be able to tell him this, Paddy? Niko had been through so much. He is so happy now, here with me."

"Let's see! This gives us two weeks, Roger. I have to be in school in a few minutes. I will come over later on. We can talk about this privately some more, when Niko has gone to bed," Father O'Mally said, squeezing Roger's shoulders.

Dinner was quiet, but Niko was so happy to see the Father, to show him his drawings, that he didn't react to Roger's bad mood. Afterward when he left for bed, the two men talked until late that night.

Father O'Mally kept silent for a few minutes before posing the question to Roger:

"How do you really feel deep down in your heart about Niko?" he asked.

"I care a great deal for the boy. I can't even think about him leaving me now. He had filled the emptiness in my heart since Monique passed away. Each day I get more involved with Niko. Now they want to take him away from me," he articulated.

Father O' Mally hesitated a few seconds before asking again.

"Tell me, Roger, how would you like to adopt Niko yourself?"

"Do you think this would be possible, Paddy?" asked Roger with hope in his voice.

Father O' Mally was silent for a few seconds. He had worked with orphans before and knew a few rules concerning adoption.

"I don't know, Roger, but if you're really sincere about adopting the boy, why don't you call the judge to find out."

"You're financially well off with your successful studio. I don't think it would be a problem in this aspect. Think about it, my friend, for this is a serious decision," the Father told him.

He could see the sadness in Roger's face. After a few seconds, Roger looked at him.

"I would love for Niko to be part of my life to if he wanted," he answered.

First thing in the morning, Roger called the judge to make the appointment. He and Patrick left for Marseille while Niko was at school. The Father wanted to stand by his friend and speak to the judge on Roger's behalf. He was concerned about the outcome.

Roger was on pins and needles all the way to Marseille. The judge saw them right away, explaining to them that the adoption papers were never signed before the family saw the orphan to be adopted.

Father O' Mally explained to him that Roger was sincere in his wish to adopt Niko. The judge was silent at first, thinking the matter thoroughly before looking at Roger.

"Adopting a child is a serious commitment of two parents. You're a widower, which means that Niko will have no mother. It's against regulation to do this.

The matter has to go before the board. I cannot give you hope that this request will be granted," he said with a grave voice which send a chill to Roger's heart.

"I can provide for Niko sufficiently, judge. I have a very good income, and plenty of love for this boy," pleaded Roger.

"We have to wait for the decision of the couple interested adopting him, and then, the decision of the board.

I will contact you if there is any change," the judge said rising from his desk. The meeting was over.

Roger felt his heart plunge to his stomach. It seemed that his legs couldn't support him. He could hardly get through the door.

He was going to lose Niko.

Chapter Fifteen

The Letter

November- December, 1952

Niko hadn't been told about the recent outlook concerning his future. Roger thought that he should wait for the judge's decision. After the trip to Marseille, Roger hadn't felt this low since the death of Monique.

He tried to concentrate on his work but his heart wasn't there. It didn't take long for Niko to notice the change in his guardian's attitude.

Usually Roger was happy, talking about many things with Niko when he came back from school.

The silence at the meal table was even worse. Norma didn't sing anymore as she always did in the kitchen.

Instead, she would look at the boy, shaking her head, and then hug him so tightly he couldn't breathe. Several times he had caught tears in her eyes. Although she still spoiled him, she was acting like Fifi after the funeral of his grandfather.

"Why is everybody so different?" he wondered.

After several days, the tension became difficult for Niko. The orphan was sure that he had done something wrong to displease Roger. He went through his days at school with a heavy heart.

During the art sessions, he did his utmost to please his guardian, thinking that he was the source of the problem. Whenever Father O' Mally saw him during school, he didn't joke with him as he always did.

It had to be his fault. He knew it.

Why would everybody be so quiet? It was worse during the weekends. Niko had always looked forward to the end of the week because Roger and he did so many things together.

He missed the closeness that they had before. The boy hid his sorrow, keeping everything to himself. He felt so alone, just like after Oppa's death.

As usual when he was suffering, he touched his medallion and turned to his Blessed Mother to confide his distress.

When he was very little, the angels, Jesus, and the Blessed Mother were real to him. They were like true family to him, but he had always favored his Blessed Mother. He loved to kook at her comforting face.

"When you're suffering too much to pray, the angels will pray for you,"

Father O' Mally had told him after his beating ordeal.

Niko thought about this during the meal with Roger, letting out a heavy sigh which suddenly brought his guardian's attention. The boy, his head down, was pushing his food around his plate. Niko used to be always hungry.

"You're not hungry tonight, Niko?" Roger asked.

"Not very much," Niko answered in a low voice, still with his head down. Roger saw immediately that something was bothering the boy.

"What's wrong, Niko? Did something happened at school today?" he asked, very concerned.

"No. It's not that," the boy answered.

"What is it, then? Do you feel sick? Let me look at you," asked Roger getting up quickly from the table to go and touch his forehead.

"No, I'm not sick," he said, struggling to hold back tears.

"It just that I don't know what I did wrong to upset you. Please tell me why you're mad, Roger," the boy said, letting tears toll down his checks.

"Dear God! I'm not mad at you, far from it. I love you Niko. You're very dear to my heart. I don't know what I'll do without you. I need you, Niko," he continued on his knees, hugging the orphan.

"Then why don't you talk to me any more ?" the boy sobbed.

"Forgive me if my thoughts were somewhere else. It has nothing to do with you disappointing me," Roger told him, hugging him again.

He suddenly realized that his dark mood had greatly affected Niko.

"I have great troubles in my mind, Niko. I'm so sorry if I hurt you. Please, forgive me and give me a big hug," Roger told him, holding him close to reassure him.

He was unable to bring himself to tell Niko the truth.

This would be disastrous to the boy after what he had gone through. It would be soon enough when it became official. Beside, he shouldn't give up hope, as Paddy told him last night. Miracles do happen.

"I Know!" he said to change the boy's state of mind.

"How would you like to go to the Christmas Fair in Marseille on Sunday, Niko? You can see an exposition of Santons just like those your grandfather used to create," he added.

"And perhaps this outing would be good for me as well," he thought to himself.

"Oh! Yes, I'd like to go there very much, Roger. Oppa used to take me with him," the boy said, his eyes lifting up. He was already feeling better.

"Good! Dry your tears. We'll go then. Christmas is coming next month you know?" he told the boy, hoping that they would be still together.

"I must get out of this depressed mood for the boy's sake. Niko is so sensitive. How could I have forgotten about this," Roger thought, ashamed of himself.

The Christmas Fair was crowded with people looking for gifts. Niko enjoyed the Santons exposition as they went from room to room. The little figurines were adorable in their peasant costumes.

The atmosphere enlivened Niko that afternoon, for he was back in his element. The colorful costumes attracted his eyes. Color was his favorite interest and once again, he remembered Oppa working in his studio, blending his colors for the Santons.

As they looked at some art painting later, Roger met several art dealers whom he knew. He was very popular among them.

"What would you like for your Christmas, Niko?" Roger asked him on their way back to the villa.

He had already had something in mind for him, but wanted to know what the boy would like. Perhaps, Niko was hoping for a special gift.

"I don't want anything but to stay with you, Roger, forever. It would be my best Christmas gift. I love you like Oppa," the little boy answered him quickly.

Trembling with emotions, Roger had to stop the car to park on the side of the road. He was speechless for a few seconds.

The boy's answer went right through his heart like an arrow. He had trouble breathing and couldn't find words to reply to this child's confession.

"You'll stay with me forever, Niko. I'll do everything in my power to make it happen," he managed to answered, holding him against his chest.

"If I had a little boy, I would love him to be just like you, Niko," he continued with teary eyes. Niko sincere confession had been so spontaneous that it took Roger by surprise.

"I don't want to go to an orphanage, ever. I want to stay here with you, Norma and Peco. You've been good to me," he said, keeping his head against Roger's chest.

He was overwhelmed by the boy's opening up in this way. Later he called Paddy to tell him about the little boy's confession.

"I pray for this door to open, Roger. Niko will need love now more than anything else you can give him," Father O' Mally told him.

"You have accomplished more than I had hoped for. This orphan boy has opened his heart to you. I couldn't do that," he added.

November went by and December came too fast. Still, there was no news from the judge. Roger, torn by his emotion and his love for Niko, did his very best not to show the boy his torment.

Days passed leaving him hopeful. He couldn't understand why he hadn't heard from the judge. Niko was due to see his adoptive family, and the waiting was nerve racking. He had called Paddy for emotional support.

Father O' Mally, understanding his friend distress, told him to pray and be patient. This type of legal procedure always took time. Perhaps it was for the best?

"Hope and prayer is the best medicine," he said, sensing his pain but unable to help his friend.

However, Father O' Mally didn't reveal his fears. He had worked with orphanage in the past and was aware of the problems which could affect the adoption. Without a mother for Niko, the board might refuse Roger. His friend was trouble enough as it was.

December 3 came. Still no news from the judge. The little village of Cassis prepared joyously for Noël. The shops were festive with decorations and illuminations in their windows for the coming event.

The small "Sainte-Marie des Pêcheurs" church was decorated by the children from school under the Sisters guidance.

Of course, Niko had participated as well in this project, making paper angels for the tree. Although Roger made a great effort to be in the mood for the boy's sake, the waiting was unbearable.

Niko unaware that his future was in the hands of fate, enjoyed the coming event of Christmas.

On December 10, before school closed for the holiday, Niko read a Christmas story to his class. At the same time, a letter to Roger finally arrived from the judge. In complete panic, Roger called Paddy, for he was too scare to open it. Could he come to see him?

Come right away, Roger. We're busy with the Christmas pageant but I have a few minutes free before lunch to see you.

Roger's heart was racing as he arrived at the Presbytery.

"I'm afraid to read it, Paddy. Could you read it for me?" he asked the Father.

Opening the envelope, the Father read the letter first to himself without looking at Roger who was sitting in agony next to him. Father O' Mally's face never betrayed what he saw through the letter. Then, after a few seconds, he read to Roger:

Dear Monsieur Gallet

I understand your urgency in whishing to known the final decision about Niko's adoption.

I apologize for the delay. The family in question changed their mind about adopting Niko.

If you are still interested in the adoption, could you please call my office at once to make an appointment to finalize the necessary documents.

Please make a note that our office will be close for the holidays next week.

Best Regards,

Judge Marchand

During the reading, Roger couldn't breathe. His heart was in his throat as Father O' Mally finished the letter, Roger stood speechless, overwhelmed with emotions. He held his friend against him with teary eyes, thanking him for his unconditional support.

"I will be Niko's legal father tomorrow," he managed to articulate. His vision was blurred by tears.

They decided to say nothing to Niko when he returned from school. The surprise should wait until tomorrow when Roger had the documents in hand.

Roger was well aware that Father O' Mally was busy with Christmas, but he begged him to come share this moment with Niko and him once the papers were ready.

"You stood by me through so much. You're part of this family, Paddy.

You must be here with us. This will be our moment," he said.

Father O' Mally didn't hide his feelings. He always had a special soft spot in his heart for Niko.

He didn't want to miss this for all the world so he promised to come for dinner the following evening. Niko would be out of school tomorrow afternoon for the two- week holiday. This would be a real celebration and a Christmas to remember.

When Roger came back from Marseille the next day, he held the envelope containing the adoption papers. He read and reread them several times.

He couldn't believe this miracle. Niko was his, his very own son.

He went into the kitchen to tell the good news to Norma. He knew how happy she would be about the outcome.

"Please, don't mention anything to Niko, yet. This is a surprise, " he warned her.

Paddy is coming for dinner with us to celebrate.

Roger held the large sealed envelope anxiously close to his heart. He had signed page after page at the judge's office that morning.

The suspense was finally over. He read the document one more time to fully understand the adoption rules.

Niko was officially his legal son and heir. He suddenly felt like a new man with a purpose. He was a father now, Niko's Father.

Norma was preparing a special dinner for tonight. Father was coming to celebrate the good news with them. They were going to tell Niko. She had trouble to containing her joy when the boy came back from school just as she was preparing the dessert.

It was almost dinner time when Father O' Mally came by. Niko, always happy to see him, noticed at once the smiling faces around him. Roger was in a great mood. Norma was singing again in the kitchen. This would be a great evening.

"There is a surprise for you, Niko, after dinner," Roger told him happily.

By the look on everybody's face, the boy guessed it would be good, and he was anxious for dinner to be over.

It wasn't his birthday. What was this surprise, anyway?

Chapter Sixteen

The Revelation

December 12, 1952.

Roger could hardly contain himself until dinner was over. Norma had outdone herself preparing Niko's favorite dessert, chocolate mousse. When the boy had finished the last mouthful, Roger looked at Father O' Mally before calling the boy.

"Niko, come seat on my knees before I tell you about your surprise. I have something very important to tell you," he said. He couldn't wait any longer.

"I went to Marseille this morning to sign an important document. From now on, we will never be separated because you belong to me. I am your father, my son," he told the boy with great emotion in his voice.

Niko went very still, looking at him, then at Father O' Mally for affirmation.

"Roger has adopted you, Niko. You don't have to be afraid of going to the orphanage anymore. You are his son and heir forever," Father O' Mally told the boy.

The speechless little boy remained still, unable to react to the news. Then, all at once, he put his arms around Roger's neck.

"I wanted you to be my father, Roger, because I love you with all my heart. I will do my best for you to be proud of me, my father," he said.

The biggest smile Father O' Mally ever saw on the boy illuminated his face.

His deep brown eyes shone with happiness. Niko then went down on his knees in front of the Father to kiss both of his hands before saying,

"Thank you Father for praying for Niko. I have asked my Blessed Mother secretly for this. It was my dearest wish and she answered my prayers."

Both men were touched by the boy's confession. Roger held the boy against him, his love for the orphan had never wavered.

What a future they would have together, for he had great plans for Niko. He had a new goal in life now. He had a son to raise.

On the following afternoon, Roger took the excited boy to look for a Christmas tree. The villa, which had never been decorated since Roger lost his wife, suddenly took on a festive look.

Just before dinner, there was a knock at the door. Norma was busy with dinner in the kitchen therefore, Roger went to open the door himself.

His joyous mood evaporated at once and his face turned to ice.

In front of him there was Gus standing on the door's steps with a small package in his hands. The man clearly had an embarrassing look about him.

"I know this is awkward, Monsieur Gallet, but I wanted to bring this for Niko. I didn't know where to find him. Pierre at the restaurant told me where to contact you.

Roger's face lost his color as the man in front of him spoke.

"I've done a terrible wrong to the boy and felt sorry ever since. I have wanted to tell this to him myself," the man said in a sorrowful voice.

"I've been dealing with a lots of problems with the business lately. When it got worse, my drinking became out of control. I've just sold the boat and the fishing business. I'm ready to move with my brother in Marseille and work with him.

I wanted to make peace with Niko before my leave."

Roger, mute by the man's confession, mellowed toward him, for he too, had been down the road before. Without his good friend Paddy, who knows what would have become of him?

He motioned for him to enter the house, and called Niko.

"Niko, can you come here for a minute? There is someone here who wishes to see you," he said.

Niko came immediately wondering who it was but his smile froze on his face when he saw Gus standing there.

"Hi there, Niko! I wanted to bring you a small peace offering to tell you how sorry I am for the way I've treated you. You were a great little worker and I can't tell you how ashamed I am for what happened between us," Gus told him, before handing Niko the small package he was holding.

Niko, accepted the gift from Gus and his smile came back once again.

"It's OK, Gus. I knew that you didn't mean it, thank you for the present," the boy told him and shook his hand before the man walked back to the door, saying his good byes.

When he opened the gift, it was a wooden pencil holder with a fish carved on the top.

"There is something good in everyone, my son," Roger told him. " It took courage to come and see you after what happened. Forgiveness is a lesson for all of us."

Roger was proud of his young son for the way he accepted Gus apologies.

After dinner that evening, Roger and Niko, trimmed the tree together with Norma's and Peco's approval.

Niko couldn't stand the anticipation, but Roger had another confession to tell the boy. It was time to tell him about his parents.

"Niko, I know this has been on your mind for a long time. Some time ago, I made you a promise which I meant to keep.

I have received the papers about the research concerning your parents. Now I want to tell you what I found," he said, knowing how troubled the boy was about his father.

Niko's excitement disappeared at once. The little face became serious while he listened attentively to Roger. Yes! He wanted this very much. He had kept this deep down in his heart since the day he found his father's picture in the hideout. He wanted to found out about his Papa.

"You should be very proud of your mother and father, Niko, for both of them were true heroes. During the war they participated in the France's liberation.

They belonged to the *"Partisans,"* who did great deed for our freedom.

In order to perform their deeds, the Partisans had to hide in the deep wilderness, sometimes in caves for a long time. They lived in the wild territories of the Calanques as well by all types of weather under terrible conditions.

What you found in the cave was real, probably part of their story, Niko.

Your grandfather told you the truth. After both of your parents died, he raised you in La Madrague were you were born.

Your parents gave their life during the great battle in Marseille so we have our freedom again. Your father was a special man, a great hero for France, one of the best. His death was mourned by many.

I wanted you to know this for it is part of your heritage, my son. I'm sure that you will learn more about the freedom of France in school. When you get older, you'll understand the price your mother and father paid for our freedom.

You can be proud of them," Roger said, once more, putting his hand on the boy's head who stood next to him quietly. Afterward, Niko ran to his room to get the cherished picture of his parents. Roger had put it in a silver frame for him.

"Thank you for telling me all this, father. Now, I understand why my father's picture was in that old newspaper in the cave. Do you think he slept there?" he asked.

"Perhaps! I guess we'll never know, Niko" he answered, holding him against him. "We will go together to visit them and your grandfather in the cemetery," he added to raise Niko's spirits.

Niko looked forward to Christmas as much as Roger. The closeness that they had developed was that of father and son. On Christmas Eve, Roger went to the village to do some shopping while Niko stayed in his room drawing.

Roger already had a special gift which he had put aside sometime ago for Niko. There was something else that he had ordered for him in Cassis the week before. He hoped that it would be ready for it was of great importance to the boy.

Norma was very busy in the kitchen preparing the Christmas meal. She had baked all types of goodies. Close to her apron, waiting for a little handout, Peco never left her side.

On Christmas morning, Roger, with his little son at his side, knelt during mass in front of the Virgin Mother's statue. He couldn't thank her enough for giving him this miracle. Niko was very quiet. His head bend down, the small boy prayed silently to her in his own way.

He had offered his unconditional love to his new father. This love which has been locked in his heart deeply since Oppa had left him.

They both wished Merry Christmas to Father O' Mally before he left to spend a few days at Kate's house for the holiday.

"I have a special gift for you to open later, Niko, the Father said, holding a package in his hands. Merry Christmas to both of you," he smiled.

After lunch at the villa, it was time to open the gifts under the tree. Niko opened Father O' Mally's gift first after reading the card on it.

"Enjoy your Christmas gift together. God works in wondrous ways."

When the boy opened the gift, it was a beautiful book with colored pictures about the Holy family. It recounted the true story of Christmas, the birth of Jesus.

Then it was Roger's turn to get his gifts for Niko from under the tree.

"Let's see what the Père Noël brought last night," he said, coming back with three packages in his hands.

"The first one is for a certain pooch," Roger said to Peco sitting in front of both of them. The pooch in question had been sniffing the tree since they had brought it in the house. For a few minutes it had worried everybody.

Who knows what the mischievous dog would do?

"It's a new collar for you, Peco, with your name and address. I think you need one now. Your old one is getting too small," he said, handling the boy the package.

Niko put the red collar around Peco's neck. The pooch no longer looked like a little mutt. With the good food and Norma's treats, he had grown so much.

"Look, Peco, at what father got for you. Now you look like a real dog," he said happily, putting the collar on his friend. The boy and the dog had gone through so much together.

"Merry Christmas, Niko, this one is for you. Open it. I think you're going to like it, my son," he told the boy with a smile.

The package contained a silver frame with the picture of his grandfather working in his studio with his Santons. Father O' Mally had asked Kate to find it through the archives in her museum. Roger had had it framed in a shop in Cassis.

Niko looked at it for a long time. His Oppa looked so happy. He studied the snow white crop of his grandfather's hair, so familiar that it bought tears to his eyes. He would put it next to his parents picture on his dresser.

"Thank you for this beautiful gift, father. I didn't have a picture of my Oppa," he told Roger, touching the frame gently with his fingers.

"I'm glad that you like it, Niko. I knew that you needed this with you.

Now, my son, open this last gift," Roger told the boy, handing him the third present, brightly wrapped with a red ribbon.

"This used to belong to me when I was your age. My father gave this to me a long time ago. I know that you will put it to good use," Roger said.

Niko opened the present, looking at his content. His deep chocolate eyes became too large for his face. He stared at the long wooden box. The old dark wood had a certain patina due to age.

This gift was more precious to him because it had belonged to his new father. So many colors neatly lined up in rows. He caressed the pastels lovingly, his small fingers relishing this moment.

Roger was moved to see the boy's fondness for the gift. He had had the hinges on the box repaired last week, and was about Niko's age the day his own father had given this to him for Christmas.

'Thank you father, this is a gift I will cherish all my life," he said putting both of his arms around Roger's neck. The boy was truly overwhelmed by this gift.

"I have something for you too, father," he said before running into his bedroom and coming back with a package wrapped in plain paper and tied with a red ribbon he had gotten from Norma.

"For my Father," he had written on the package.

"This is for you, my father," handing him the gift and referring to him proudly as *"My Father."*

Roger was touched by the boy's gift when he opened it.

Niko had spent many hours secretly finishing it since their trip to the Christmas fair in Marseille.

It was a drawing representing a small boy with his dog sitting by him on a hill. The boy had his back turned, looking at the crimson sunset, plunging down toward the cobalt sea.

Niko's loneliness in the drawing was exceptionally moving and so well shown. The sight of these two souls in the wilderness moved Roger deeply. He would remember this forever. He remained silent for a few seconds, looking at the drawing.

"Do you like my drawing, father?" Niko finally asked, waiting for Roger to speak.

"OH! I like it very much, Niko. You achieved a masterpiece. It needs to be framed. Nothing could please me more than this gift, created by your own hands, my son. Thank you for this," he said hugging the boy.

His little genius had created the details so perfectly, describing his feelings with his fingers better than words could.

That first Christmas together was very special for the father and the son. Through this bond, they had found a special gift that both of them had lost for a while.

The gift of love had been buried deep in their heart for them to retrieve. Roger remembered a poem he had read somewhere a long time ago;

"The love in your heart is not there to stay.
This love in your heart is there to be given away"

The End

(m) indicates masculine gender, (f) feminine gender and (pl) plural.

Bambino (m) - little one

Barbe à Papa (f) - cotton - candy

Bar de La Marine (m) - sailor's bar

Belle Sardine (f) - beautiful sardine

Bonelli Eagle (m)- diurnal birds, most rare endangered species -(about 15 pairs left)

Bouillabaise (f) - famous traditional Provencal safron-flavored seafood soup

Boulangerie (f)- bread shop

Bourride (f)- thick fish soup served with special sauce to dip bread into

Calanques (f) - spectacular sea-eroded gashes in high, limestone cliffs covered with dense-areas of wilderness

Calissons (m) - sweet confection made out of almond paste covered with icing

Chamomille (f) medicinal herb used in tea and beauty products

Chanterelle (f) - thin strand of violin string that produces a rasping sound, poetically called the cicada's song

Château d' îf (m)- massive old fortress in the sea similar to Alcatraz prison. (See the Comte-de -Monte-Cristo novel)

Capelino (m)- Provencal head's covering bonnet bonnet for young ladies

Criée (f)- (la criée), used by fishmongers selling fish on the market

Dia (m) meaning God or dear God (Irish)

Farandole (f) - middle-age Mediterranean danced to a six-beats rhythm

Fennel (m)- sweet vegetable root flavor tasting like anis

Fish Mongers (pl) market fish-sellers

Fishu (m) - head scarf cover made of lace

Foigme -Cara (m) - we're almost there, (Irish)

Fjords -(pl)- under water valleys shaped by glaciers

Fougasse- (m)- rich, flat olive bread

Galoubet (m) - small 3-holes flute producing a piercing sound

Garrigues (pl) - heather-carpeted dense bushes, widespread in the Calanques.

Grotte - Cosquer (f)- underwater cave with hand prints and animal drawings dating approximately one or two millennia.

Guardian (m)- tutor-mentor, often, person in charge of orphan

La Madrague (f) - author used it for Niko's estate. (Originally a village near Marseille)

Maquis (m)- area of cliffs, caves and dense shrubbery area used during W. W. II by the Partisans underground Resistance attached to General De Gaulle &Allies

Médaillon (m) - biblical medals

Mimosa (m)- Mediterranean heavily, perfumed flourish tree

Mistral (m)- bitter, incessant dry, north wind in southern France

Moules Marinière (f)- famous French, creamy, mussels dish cooked in wine

Mousse au Chocolat (f)- chocolate mousse

Navettes (pl) - Provencal famous, orange- scented, small, boat-like biscuits

One -Hundred-Year-War (f)- (1337-1453) England against France bringing famine & Bubonic plague in the wake of Black Death

Pain Bagnat (m) - Provencal bread-roll filled with tuna, tomatoes, onion, pressed down.

Partisans (pl)- freedom fighters group attached to Allies underground during W.W.II

Père Noël (m)- Santa Claus (French)

Pétanque (f)- Provencal game played on sandy ground. Very heated when players measured marks with a small measure tape

Pissaladière (f)- pizza with anchovy and onion topping

Ratatouille (F)- famous Mediterranean stew made of seafood & vegetables from the region.

Sainte- Marie-des-Pêcheurs
(f)- church named after Virgin to protect fishermen

Santons (pl) - originally biblical clay colorful little figurines created for Christmas. They became popular in Provence, representing baker, miller, milkmaid, etc. (Golden craft for Collectors)

Scaler (m) - to scale fish

Soupe au Pistou (f) - locale dish made out of vegetables, noodle, beans, basil, garlic

Studio (m)- workplace often used by artist to paint or carve their work

Tea-Rose Hybrids (f) - crossed-bride type of roses, usually of pale, pinkish hues

Tambourinaire (pl)- person playing drum

Tisane (f)- medicinal herbal tea

Vieux-Port (m)- ancien port section, related to Phocaeans (600 BC) landing galleys in Massalia (Marseille)

Vin-du-Pays (m)- locale wine of the region

LaVergne, TN USA
26 November 2009

165357LV00002B/1/P